hot SECRETS

TALL, DARK
AND
DEADLY SERIES

LISA RENEE JONES

Hot Secrets
by Lisa Renee Jones

Book 1 of the New York Times bestselling
TALL, DARK, AND DEADLY series

The Tall, Dark, and Deadly series includes:
Book 1: Hot Secrets
Book 2: Dangerous Secrets
Book 3: Beneath the Secrets

Also by Lisa Renee Jones

The Inside Out Series
If I Were You
Being Me
Revealing Us
His Secrets*
Rebecca's Lost Journals
The Master Undone*
My Hunger*
No In Between
My Control*
I Belong to You
All of Me*

The Secret Life of Amy Bensen
Escaping Reality
Infinite Possibilities
Forsaken
Unbroken*

Careless Whispers
Denial
Demand (May 2016)
Surrender (December 2016)

Dirty Money
Hard Rules (August 2016)
More information coming soon…

*eBook only

The Walker Brothers...

Tall, dark, and deadly, these three brothers run Walker security. Each brother is unique in his methods and skills, but all share key similarities. They are passionate about those they love, relentless when fighting for a cause they believe in, and believe that no case is too hard, no danger too dark. Dedication is what they deliver, and results are their reward.

PROLOGUE

He sat at the Manhattan coffee bar in a dark corner, his back to the wall, his laptop on the wooden table, when the waitress set his coffee down and quickly departed without a word. The oversized white mug rested on a saucer and held plain black coffee. He didn't believe in flavors and sweet things, unless they came in the form of soft, womanly curves, the kind he liked to have beneath him, on top of him, and then quickly out of the way. Used and disposed of, and therefore incapable of creating problems he didn't need, or want, in his life.

Discreetly, he snagged the small data stick that the waitress had slipped onto the saucer, popped it into his computer, and took a sip of hot coffee.

A few punches on his keyboard and the image of the familiar auburn-haired female who'd become the reason he lived, the reason he got up every day, along with details of her habits, memberships, likes and dislikes, appeared on the screen. Details on a wire to his offshore account scrolled across the page. His gaze shifted to the table directly across from his, and he almost laughed at the assumption that he could be bought, that he wanted the paycheck offered. This was about so much more than money. Because at that table, so close he could almost smell the vanilla scent of the shampoo he knew she kept on the edge of her shower, was his target, a delicate little flower, even if she didn't know it, even if she played tough in the courtroom. But she'd know when he was done with her. She'd know, because he was going to tear her apart, one petal at a time, and relish every moment of it, too. He'd profiled her, just as she profiled the suspects in the cases she took to trial for the District Attorney's office. After all, he didn't earn the nickname 'Dirt Diver' without merit. And just as his target used her suspects' habits, and their perceived weaknesses against them in court, he'd use hers against her. He'd taunt her, announce he was coming for her, and watch her pretend indifference, watch her stupidly stand alone. He was going to touch her world as she'd touched his. Draw out her torture, make her scream his name. Make her beg for her life. And then, and only then, he would kill her.

ONE

"What you need is a man."

Lauren Reynolds groaned at her best friend's far too loudly spoken suggestion, feeling as if one of the elegant chandeliers of the fancy New York ballroom had just become a spotlight. "Keep your voice down before someone hears you."

"Touchy, touchy." Julie chided, her baby blue eyes brimming with as much mischief as the deep V of her sparkling blue gown. "Why do you care what these people think?"

"I have to care, and you know it. *These people* are my father's friends and colleagues, who happen to be here to celebrate his birthday. And enough with this 'you need a man' stuff you've been harping on all week. We can't all be Marilyn Monroe look-a-likes who can thumb through men like a mailbox full of advertisements. I guess blondes do have more fun and us brunettes are stuck with chocolate and Marie Claire magazines."

"How very boring."

"Boring works for me. Between my father's career and my work, I'm up to my neck with male egos and still sinking."

Julie set her glass down on one of the several bars in a spacious room with tables filled with delicate finger foods, and plenty of spotlight chandeliers dangling above them. "Finally, we get to the root of the problem. Clearly, you've been locked up and sheltered in your daddy's world too long. You've forgotten real men are not politicians."

"I work for the District Attorney's office, Julie." Lauren bristled. "I'm about to go to trial on a murder case with the death penalty on the table, and it won't be my first. I hardly call that 'locked up and sheltered.' And I'm hardly surrounded by nothing but politicians."

"Oh, please. Not only is the DA an elected position, this particular DA is all about playing the game of politics, and *you* know that." Julie studied Lauren a moment, her expression and tone softening before she added, "Look, honey, your lack of male companionship aside, I'm worried about my best friend. You need to get some rest and have some fun. Ever since you started prepping for this trial, you've been working around the clock. And before this one, there was another."

"This one is big," Lauren argued. "It's—"

"They're *all* big to you," Julie said. "That's why you're getting assigned murder cases, not petty theft cases. You work insane hours without complaint, then pull 'daughter' duty like some sort of robot."

"It's his birthday, Julie."

"Tonight I understand," she said. "It's the many other functions and I do mean *many* that he insists you attend, that you need to put a stop to." She lowered her head and softened her voice. "You need a life that isn't his, which brings me back to the 'hot male' category of this conversation, and no, I'm not talking the email version."

"I just got out of a relationship. I don't need another."

"You didn't *just* get out of anything. You dumped your cheating ex-fiancé, who was hotter for your father's power than he was you, more than six months ago. And not without bruises to your emotions and your confidence, which makes me want to find the man and give him a good knee to the balls. I'll just settle for helping you get back on the horse."

"Julie," she ground out. "I'm going to hurt you if you don't zip it."

"You're beautiful and sexy," she said, as if Lauren hadn't even spoken, "and he made you feel like Ugly Betty when you're Audrey freaking Hepburn. You need a hot man to carry you away and remind you that you are more than the sum of a courtroom or your father's career aspirations on your behalf."

Lauren snorted at that. "With my luck, I'd choose an undercover reporter who'd twist me into some sort of floozy, which would spiral into a scandal for my father."

Julie's eyes brightened mischievously and then widened with delight at her own thoughts. "Actually, Lauren, maybe that's just what you *need*."

"What the heck does that mean?" Lauren asked, frowning, pretty sure she knew what was coming. The push. Julie loved "the push," what she called her closing arguments on anything, in or out of a courtroom.

"Your father's about to retire, but he has that Kennedy family grandeur in his sights. He wants you to run for office. He's not going to give up until he convinces you." Her eyes twinkled with mischief. "So you see, a scandal can't really hurt *him*, but it could help *you dodge a political bullet*."

Lauren grimaced. "Apparently you've broken our golden rule of sobriety in public and had too much bubbly, because you're talking craziness. I work for the District Attorney's office. I have my own career to think about, too, and you know it."

Julie pursed her perfect lips. "I don't know anything of the sort. It's not like you want to run for DA any more than you want to run for any other appointed office. And you're in the public sector with a conviction rate that's well above expectations, so you're a golden girl."

"Any scandal I bring to the office, I bring to the DA. Not to mention, I'm not exactly the scandal kind of girl."

"Oh, good grief," Julie grumbled. "I was just baiting you with the whole scandal thing, but the fact that you didn't even get that is telling, and of what, I'm not sure."

There was an announcement at the front of the room, something about cake and presents in half an hour. Lauren skimmed her hand down her out-of-character siren-red silk gown, her gaze catching on the dainty, silver watch on her wrist, the newest in a broad collection of gifts from her father. Apologies for working late, missing birthdays and any number of other things. She wondered what had earned her a gift on his birthday, and when she'd find out.

Julie touched her arm. "You okay?"

Lauren inhaled and let it out. "Fine. I'm fine. I just need more champagne."

"Looking for a little tolerance for step-mommy dearest, I take it?"

"Don't you know it," Lauren agreed, dreading the inevitable 'make-nice moments' with her father's trophy wife.

"Well, to heck with our sobriety pact," Julie declared. "A bubbly dose of patience, coming right up."

Several minutes later, Lauren sipped from a flute and waved

at one of her father's friends across the room. She wondered if the man really was a friend, or just someone jockeying for some position.

Julie leaned in close. "Oh honey, you're waving at an old fuddy-duddy, so I've just waved my magic wand. I have the perfect male specimen to carry you away to orgasmic bliss. Mr. Make Every Woman Hot And Bothered himself is in the house."

"I seem to remember you inferring only minutes ago that there were no men capable of such splendor at these types of events."

"He's your 'midnight fantasy,'" she said, a wicked smile on her lips. "Or so a certain brunette told me just last weekend, after a few glasses of wine."

Royce Walker. She was talking about *Royce Walker*. Lauren's throat went dry at the mention of the sexy State Security Advisor, who also ran a private security company with his two brothers. And, most definitely, had been the object of her 'midnight fantasies' on more than one occasion. "He's here tonight?"

"Over here, Royce!" Julie called out and then grinned. "He's not only here, he's headed our way. You can thank me later."

"Oh dear God, Julie," Lauren chided. "Why did you do that? I have enough stress tonight without this." And damn it, she needed a little fantasy here and there. She didn't want it ruined by real life.

"If you won't take care of you, honey," Julie said, reaching out and tugging Lauren's bodice down an inch, "I will."

"Good evening, ladies," Royce greeted her from behind, his voice as rawly masculine as one would expect from a man with a body of a god and long raven hair he'd regretfully tied at his nape for an event such as this one.

Lauren pulled up her dress, and shot Julie a warning look. "We'll be talking later."

"Of course," Julie said with a grin a moment before Royce stepped between them, towering over them. "Hey there, Royce."

Lauren turned fully to greet him, having only an instant to take in his tuxedo, which fit him to perfection, before her gaze collided with his crystal blue stare. "Hello," he said, his voice lower now, almost intimate.

"Hello," she said, willing herself to say something more, but the unexpected direct eye contact sizzled her all the way to her toes and apparently stole her ability to process words.

"Shouldn't you be somewhere keeping your brothers out of trouble?" Julie asked him.

"As tedious and impossible as that is," he said, "it would be more pleasant than rubbing elbows with a bunch of wannabe movers and shakers. But duty sometimes requires a tuxedo and nerves of steel."

Lauren gaped, her reaction instantaneous, her processing skills fully recovered. She might not approve of her father wholeheartedly, but she loved him. "You do know this is my father's birthday party, right?"

"Ah," Julie said. "I think I should say 'Oops' here because I thought you two had officially met. I'm assuming that's not the case."

Royce's far too sensual lips curved slightly. "Nice to finally meet you 'officially,' Ms. Reynolds," he said, extending his hand to Lauren. "Though we've certainly crossed paths at a few events."

She ignored his hand. "You knew who I was, but you still

made that comment about my father's party?"

"When your father invited me here tonight, I suggested he cancel this monkey-suit event and have a family barbecue," he said. "I even offered to bring the beer and my brothers for entertainment. He wasn't interested. So yes, I knew who you were when I made the comment."

"You told my father…" She shook her head. "Did you really?"

He held up two fingers. "Scout's honor. And while I was never a scout, I was in the FBI for 7 years, so that's close enough."

"And how did my father reply to your suggestion?"

"He told me to 'wear the damn monkey-suit and get your ass to my party.'"

She laughed. "Oh my God. That's so my father. You really did tell him that."

"I'm not known for my decorum, not even when I was a hostage negotiator." He held out his hand. "Shall we try again? Nice to meet you, Ms. Reynolds."

She liked him. He was so different from, well, everyone else here, and actually, quite like Julie. She slipped her palm against his, unprepared for the instant tingling awareness that rushed up her arm. "Lauren," she managed, and to her dismay, her voice cracked. "Call me…Lauren."

He brought her knuckles to his lips, his gorgeous blue eyes lifting to hers. "Lauren," he repeated softly, before releasing her hand, and man, oh man, she wanted him to touch her again like she'd never wanted to be touched before.

"I see someone I need to talk to," Julie said. "I'll be back in a few." With a turn, and a covert wink at Lauren that said she'd just made up the 'someone to talk to' as an excuse to leave Lauren alone with Royce, she disappeared.

Royce leaned an elbow on the bar. "How long have you two been friends?"

"Five years," she said, happy to have a comfortable subject to talk about. "We met our last year of law school." Lauren pushed herself up on a bar stool and crossed her legs, her dress riding up a bit above the knee, which she quickly righted.

Royce's eyes dropped to follow the action, and a combination of nervousness and awareness rushed over her. "You two seem very different," he commented, his gaze lifting to hers, his elbow settling on the bar.

"And that's bad?"

"Not bad," he said. "Just unique. Typically people are who they hang out with. But I guess you're both attorneys, so that's a common denominator."

"I know plenty of attorneys I wouldn't give the time of day to," Lauren corrected. "Julie and I share basic values about what is right and wrong and a passion for helping people. Those things are more common denominators for us than one piece of paper that says we get to practice law."

He arched a brow. "Isn't she a divorce attorney?"

"She's passionate about getting people out of bad marriages and into a new life. It's not always *what* you do to make a difference, it's that you really try to make a difference."

"Sounds like a perfect campaign pitch to me."

"And let me guess," she said dryly. "You heard I was running for office from my father." He gave a quick nod, and she shook her head. "Of course you did. I love my father, and I've supported his career, and I don't regret that. But no matter how much he commands me to run for office, it simply isn't going to happen. As in, *ever*. Under no circumstances." She lowered her voice. "My life has been completely my father's in so many ways because of his public position. That ends the day he leaves his office. You have no idea how much I crave that day." The confession was out before she could stop it. She had no idea why she had revealed such a thing to this man, this stranger, but it was done and there was no turning back.

He stared down at her, studying her with unnerving intensity, as if he was reading her soul. He, and her confession, were inescapable. And so she found herself doing the same with him, openly assessing this man she found so alluringly different from anyone she'd ever been with before. The air expanded around them, shifted, thickened. The rest of the room faded away, lost to a sudden, intense crackle of electricity. "I think," he said softly, "that I'd like to know more about you, Lauren Reynolds."

Something wonderful, wild, *and* wicked stirred inside her with his words, with the heat in his expression—something wild, wicked, and oh so unfamiliar. This man didn't fit that 'safe' profile she'd gravitated toward because it was expected of her. There was nothing safe about him, and a lot of that was exciting. But the idea of acting on her feelings sent a rush of tension through her. She bit her lip and cut her gaze to his chest. She might be confident in a courtroom, but she wasn't Julie; she wasn't a seductress who knew how to bring a man to his knees. She had Royce Walker's attention and she didn't know what to do with it.

Royce leaned closer, the spicy male scent of him flaring and filling her nostrils, and she fought the unexpected urge to reach out and touch him. "Am I making you nervous, Lauren?"

Her chin lifted, her gaze fixing on his, shocked that he'd read her so accurately. "You really do say whatever you're thinking, don't you?

"Is there a reason to do otherwise?"

She liked the answer. "You don't make me nervous." And he didn't. She was insecure in ways she didn't want to be, that she'd tried desperately to overcome since her broken engagement. But in the end, she was left afraid to believe anyone was authentic ever again, especially this man, who felt more real than any she'd ever met.

He searched her face a moment, and then offered her his hand. "Then dance with me."

Before she could think to object, if she even would have, he was leading her toward the center of the room. Anticipation pulsed through her like a live charge. She was going to dance with Royce Walker, to feel his big body pressed close to hers, and she was pretty certain it would be politically incorrect to melt into a puddle of warm, wanting female in the center of her father's birthday party. She was also pretty sure it was going to happen anyway.

***

Easing through the crowd, Royce repeated Lauren Reynolds' words in his head. *You have no idea how much I crave that day.* She had no idea, all right. No idea how much *he* craved *her*. How enticed he was by her gorgeous pale skin, by the idea of stripping her naked and caressing that skin, tasting it, feeling every inch of it, and her, molded against him. Or how enticed he was by the way her eyes danced with little yellow flecks of color when she felt strongly about something she was saying. He wondered how they would look when she was aroused and wanting. Would they be greener? Darker?

They cleared the path to the dance floor, and Royce eased Lauren onto the tiled circle where random couples moved together to an orchestra number. He braced himself for the impact of touching her, then pulled her into his arms. Their eyes collided. The mutual attraction they shared that had passed between them in passing glances over the months since he'd taken a public position, wrapped them in warmth. But he'd known it would. On some level he'd always known this woman would impact him, that she would stir something inside him he wasn't sure he remembered existing or feeling. What he'd not felt long before he'd joined the FBI fifteen years ago, when life inside the bureau had been everything, and yet somehow nothing. There was no denying that since he'd taken a more public role to promote Walker Security, the business he and his brothers ran, he'd been drawn to her each time their paths had crossed, no matter how casually or indirectly. Yet, he'd resisted approaching her, all too aware that he didn't fit into her political world, that his step into the realm of politics was merely a business endeavor, while hers was a lifestyle. That was, until tonight, when she'd declared this world to be her father's, not her own, and made it clear that everything he'd assumed about her had been wrong. Now tonight, life had pulled them together for all the wrong reasons.

She was small and soft in his arms, and nervous as hell no matter how much she denied it. And while he didn't want to make her nervous, he liked knowing he affected her, though he shouldn't, because she was off limits. He had no business flirting with her, no business wanting her, and he knew that. And yet, he couldn't seem to stop himself.

She melted against him, her head settling on his chest, the soft vanilla and honey scent of her warming him inside out. He squeezed his eyes shut, despising his reason for being here tonight, but incapable of regretting that she was in his arms. He knew she wouldn't stay there long, that she couldn't stay there long. Because the minute he'd said 'yes' to this assignment, Royce had said 'no' to Lauren.

CHAPTER
TWO

Dancing with Royce Walker, there was no denying the simple truth. He did it for her. And whatever *it* was, *it* had her body tingling and her blood pumping at lightning speed. She not only wanted this man, for once in her life she wanted more than the fantasy of being more like Julie. For once, for one night, she wanted to let go, go where desire led her, where this man would take her.

His lips brushed her ear. "You smell amazing."

Lauren's lashes fluttered before she looked up at him. There was something so powerful, so provocative about this man. She liked to be in control, normally resisted giving it away, which was one of the reasons the courtroom appealed to her. There she was respected, in charge and without her father's influence. Royce wouldn't let her have control. She knew this instinctively, but somehow didn't care. Royce's power was all his own, not bought or jockeyed for, a lethal quality she found alluring and sexy. A power he owned naturally, like a second skin that simply existed as he did. And she wasn't going to let this night with him escape because of her insecurity.

She swallowed against the dryness in her throat. "You asked

if you scare me."

His gaze dropped to her lips, and lifted. "Actually, I asked if I was making you nervous, not scared."

"Right. No. You don't make me nervous. And you don't scare me." She allowed herself the freedom, the luxury, to run her hand discreetly across one of his broad shoulders and then down his arm, loving the feel of his muscles under the tuxedo. It was bold for her to do so in public, at one of her father's events, yet all she was thinking about was how every inch of this man was hard, male perfection. "But I think *I* might be scaring me."

His hands tightened on her waist and his eyes narrowed. "Explain." He pulled her a bit closer. "What's wrong, Lauren?" He stopped dancing and just stared down at her with intense, probing eyes. "What are you telling me?" Desire spiked between them, and then lingered, a fine mist that seemed to travel over her entire body.

His reaction overwhelmed her, and sent a dash of uncertainty through her. What had made her think she could pull off the coy, flirty thing? She wasn't Julie. She knew how to play the courtroom game. The bedroom variety was another story. "Nothing. I... It was silly. Forget I said anything."

Abruptly, Royce took her hand and led her off the dance floor, forcing her to double-step to keep pace in high heels. Too quickly, before she could gain her wits back, Royce had her in a corner, where she leaned against the wall as he rested a shoulder next to her. He was so close and so big that she was successfully blocked from the view of the room.

Looking up at him, feeling a bit intimidated as he towered over her, and a lot nervous about his reaction to her words, she questioned him, "Royce?"

His voice was raspy when he spoke, urgent and oddly edgy, his eyes so intense she felt they might burn her skin. "What are you saying to me, Lauren? Is something scaring you? Is there something you need to tell—"

"No," she said quickly, thinking again how terribly, horribly bad she was at seduction. The man now thought she was in some sort of danger. "I mean yes." She'd gone this far, she wasn't going to back down. Not when Royce Walker had her trapped in a small corner and she liked it so very, very much. Lauren reached out, forcing herself to act on her desire to touch him, flattening her hand on his deliciously perfect chest. *Inhibitions be damned*, she vowed. "I...want..."

"You want what?"

"You." Oh my God, had she really just said that?

His eyes narrowed, his voice lowering an octave. "Are you saying that scares you?"

"In a good way," she admitted softly, then louder, "In a good way.

Suddenly Julie's voice broke into their exchange. "Sorry to break up the party, but it's cake time, and everyone is looking for Lauren."

Lauren could have screamed at her friend's untimely interruption.

Royce seemed to agree, flicking a quick look over his shoulder and saying, rather than asking, "Give us one minute."

Julie cleared her throat. "Hurry." And then she was gone.

Royce fixed Lauren with a probing stare, his eyes roaming her face, searching, his expression giving away nothing. "You'd better go be with your father. We'll talk afterwards."

Her heart thundered in her chest, and real fear, the kind

made of rejection, balled in her chest. No way was she going to wonder what he meant through the rest of the party. "There's nothing to talk about. You want me or you don't. Which is it, Royce?"

His reply came in actions, not words. He tipped his head down and brushed his lips across hers. The touch was brief, but somehow possessive and powerful, and a shiver of pure arousal charged down her spine and spread to other, much more intimate places.

"Oh, I want you," he said, his voice whiskey rough, where it had been a cool breeze only moments before. "Which is exactly why we need to talk."

Her stomach lurched. Not the 'talk' thing again. Why did they need to talk? Talking was what she wanted to avoid. She needed an escape, not an inquiry.

Royce surprised her and laughed. "Stop frowning." He chucked her lightly on the chin. "Go celebrate with your father so we can get out of here." His mouth was so near her ear, she felt the warmth of his breath. "*Together,* Lauren."

***

Ten minutes later, Lauren was on stage in the front of the room, trying to focus on her father and the birthday gifts he was opening, not on Royce and what would come after the party. But truth be told, her father's public persona meant far more to him than she did. Oh, he wanted her here, and he wanted her to run for office, but only because it was good for his image, for his politics, for that damn dynasty he, and his father before him who'd also been a politician, aspired to create. And because her political career would keep him in the spotlight without the pressure of holding office.

As usual, her stepmother Sharon stood quietly by his side, her long brown hair swept into an elegant knot at her neck, her exotic features carefully crafted into a mask of happiness and dedication. The press loved her. Her husband adored her for all the wrong reasons.

Sharon's gaze rushed over Lauren and she moved toward her, her clingy light blue dress bringing to mind the word *inappropriate*. She was so tired of that word, but the truth was, Sharon *was* inappropriate. Sharon knew it too, and she knew Lauren knew it. It was her father who didn't seem to see things clearly. Mr. Practical and Conservative looked the other way for a set of surgically enhanced breasts that made him feel vibrant and young.

"Lauren, dear," Sharon drawled, stepping to her side. "You seem distracted."

Lauren's teeth ground together but she managed a nonchalant shrug. "You know how I feel about these events."

Sharon cast her a reprimanding look. "This *event*, as you call it, is your father's birthday party."

Lauren fought the childish urge to roll her eyes, and with it, the pang of hurt inside her, a longing for the family she'd once had, and lost. "I'm going to suggest we have a backyard picnic or intimate dinner next year. You know, the normal things *families* do."

Sharon smiled, smugness radiating off her like a second skin. "We're not most families, and thank God for it."

"Exactly my point," Lauren mumbled and accepted a champagne flute from a waiter, feeling Royce's hot stare without even looking at him. But she knew he was in the far corner, leaning on the bar, waiting for her. She tipped her wrist back to drink and silently vowed that tonight was about indulging, about living a little.

"I see you received the watch," Sharon said, glancing at Lauren's wrist. "At least thank us for it."

Lauren didn't bother commenting. Sharon would never understand the difference between giving love and buying it. "Where is my *dear* brother Brad?" she asked instead, unable to stop the intended jab from slipping past her lips. She didn't like Sharon's son any more than she liked Sharon. He'd been eighteen and Lauren seventeen when her father had remarried, not three years after her mother's cancer had shattered her world, and though they were siblings by marriage, his creepy flirtation had been almost instant. Now, seven years later, nothing had changed.

"Brad," Sharon replied, "is off taking depositions in an important case for your father's firm, and your father would expect nothing less. In case you forgot, he runs it now, after you refused the job." Sharon's eyes darted toward Royce. "I see you have caught the eye of the oldest Walker brother. You should be more discreet."

No, Lauren thought, downing the rest of her champagne. She was tired of discreet. Really darn tired of it *and* Sharon. She might have said as much, had Sharon stayed by her side one more second.

Lauren's gaze immediately sought Royce's and found it. He was watching her exchange with Sharon. He knew they'd fought, she realized. He was too attentive not to have noticed. And oddly, considering the man was a complete stranger, she had this sense that if she needed him, he was primed and ready to act, to be there for her. For a girl who normally valued her independence, Lauren was shocked to find that idea beyond sexy, while still dipping into the realm of being downright comforting. And for the first time all week, she let herself admit that she'd been feeling uneasy, like she needed to look over her shoulder, for no explainable reason. Correction, Lauren thought. No explainable reason besides the obvious: she was preparing for a murder trial and dealing with her stepmother in the same two week span. If those two things didn't deserve a dose of comfort Royce Walker style, she didn't know what else did.

***

If Royce had ever seen a woman looking for escape, it was Lauren. She didn't like the politics of her father's world, nor most definitely her stepmother's disposition. It was clear to him that Lauren was realizing that she had no real control, that it all belonged to her father. She wanted out, was desperately yearning for freedom. He'd spent years as a hostage negotiator, seen how people dealt with the feeling of being trapped, of having all control stripped from them. So when Royce watched Lauren reach for yet another glass of champagne, he knew she was in trouble. He knew she never had more than one drink. He knew a lot about Lauren that he'd venture to say she didn't want him to know. Most importantly, he knew it was time to escort her home before she did something she'd regret in the morning.

He shoved off the bar, intending to go after her, when Lauren headed down the stairs, and began weaving or rather wobbling her way in his direction. In several long strides, Royce was in front of her, gently shackling her arms to steady her. Her hand went to her forehead, distress in her delicate features.

She looked at him with wide eyes. "Thanks. I think."

"You drank too much." He kept his voice low, and then leaned down near her ear, and whispered. "Perhaps regretting the invitation you gave me earlier?"

He felt her shiver, and then watched defiance flash in her eyes. "No. I'm not." She paused. "It's not you. It's me." She let out a breath. "It's my stepmother. It's the party. It's my… I'm rambling and I never ramble, but I'm only a little bit tipsy. That doesn't mean I don't know what I am doing, though. I do."

She might know what she was doing, but that didn't mean she wouldn't regret her actions in the morning. He wasn't in the habit of causing regret in women, and he wasn't going to start with Lauren. The best thing he could do was get her home safely, and walk away. *Lord, please give me the will to do that and nothing more.* "Did you drive to the party?"

She shook her head. "I'm a sensible subway and taxi girl. I won't pay to park a car I barely drive."

"That leaves you with two options to get home. I can get you a taxi or I can drive you home." He wanted her to say 'taxi,' for her sake, for his. But he couldn't let that be her answer, not and do his job. He needed to be her ride, to get to her home, to get closer to her.

She didn't blink, didn't look away, her voice soft and raspy, and oh so sexy as she said, "You know I want you to take me home."

The obvious reiteration of the earlier invitation he couldn't accept, no matter how much he wanted to, punched him in the gut. "Consider me your ride then."

A few minutes later, the two of them stood in the lobby of the hotel while a valet pulled his truck to the bottom of several flights of outdoor steps. He slipped his arm around her waist and they headed into the unseasonably cool April evening air. They managed to make it as far as the bottom of the first set of stairs on the terrace area when they were suddenly swarmed by reporters. Cameras flashed and microphones were shoved in their direction.

"Ms. Reynolds, how do you feel about the Sheridan execution?"

"Ms. Reynolds, tell us about your new murder trial."

"Ms. Reynolds, do you consider yourself a legal vigilante?"

"What is Senator Reynolds' feeling on the death penalty?"

Lauren tried to hide from the flashes.

"Get back," Royce ordered. "Leave her alone." He bent close to Lauren's ear. "Just keep walking, and stay close."

Someone stuck a microphone in Royce's face. "Who are you? Are you her date?"

They were only a few steps from his truck when something ice cold splattered all over them. Lauren jumped and screamed. Several reporters cursed. Royce didn't take time to consider what had been thrown or if there was real danger. Instinct and training had taught him to assume the worst, and act.

He yanked the passenger door open and helped Lauren inside the vehicle. At that moment, an egg smacked into the panel beside him and Lauren gasped at the thump. "What was that?" she asked, leaning toward him. He eased her back into her seat.

"Stay inside," was his only reply, before he shut her inside the vehicle.

The hair on the back of Royce's neck lifted as he moved to the driver's side, and climbed inside the cab. The FBI had taught him to never ignore his instincts, and his instincts were screaming of trouble where he might otherwise find only irritation.

He locked the doors and started the engine. "You okay?" he asked, glancing Lauren's way as he maneuvered them onto the highway.

She ignored his question. "That was an egg that hit your truck, wasn't it?"

"It'll wash off."

"We should go to a car wash before it destroys your paint job. I feel horrible about this, Royce." She pressed her fingers to her temple. "You have no idea how much I want to wash the cobwebs from my brain right now while we're at it."

"Hey," he said, squeezing her hand. "It's not your fault, sweetheart. You don't control what people do."

"But I should have considered how I might put you in the line of fire. And I would have, had I not stupidly drank too much champagne, which is not like me, by the way. I have a murder trial starting in two weeks, and when I juggle a high profile case, on top of the attention I get because of my father, it can get intense. I feel really, really horrible that I dragged you into my mess."

"You said that already," he said. "My truck will be fine. Stopping somewhere will only make us a target for ambitious reporters who might be following." Or someone else who intended for them to stop, and intended to take advantage of the seclusion of a late night car wash.

"I'm willing to take the risk to save your truck."

"I'm not and I have insurance for a reason."

She hesitated and nodded, then touched her dress and smelled her fingers. "Champagne. I think someone threw champagne at us. Either that or I spilled it on myself and I'm tipsier than I remember. But then, drunks don't remember, now do they?"

"You're not a drunk, and don't put yourself down for relaxing a little. And yes, what was thrown on us was champagne, which is far better than getting hit with an egg."

"Yes," she agreed. "I guess there's that to cling to." She hesitated, then said, "Maybe it's the tipsy part of this equation for me, but that scene back there rattled me way more than it normally would." She shivered and hugged herself. "I've been around my share of creepy bad guys and I got that same feeling of malice rolling off the crowd."

"It's called a typical Friday night in Manhattan," he said lightly, not about to tell her he'd felt it too, and because he wasn't supposed to know where she lived, he added, "I need your address for the GPS." She murmured a reply and he punched the information into the program. "Why don't you rest your eyes until we get there?"

She nodded and slid down into the seat, a little too willing to do as he suggested from what he knew of her personality. She was rattled all right. She knew she was in trouble.

THREE

Fifteen minutes later, Royce had paid the doorman a hefty tip to park his truck without hassle. Now on the fifth floor of the twenty-story Upper West Side residential building Lauren lived in, he waited while she fished a key out of the small beaded purse she'd gotten from the coat clerk back at the hotel. She produced a silver key chain which she proceeded to drop to the ground.

Royce scooped it up. "Let me," he offered, and when she nodded, crossing her arms in front of her, he couldn't help but notice how adorably nervous and vulnerable she appeared. He was being allowed to see what he doubted many had before him. This was a glimpse of what lay beneath the confident Assistant DA's public persona, and it was so much more than what he gambled on. Lauren wasn't a spoiled senator's daughter, or even an arrogant public servant with too much power, as he imagined she might be. She was so much deeper, so much more than her beauty, and she didn't even seem to recognize it.

He slipped the key into the lock and shoved open the door, flipping on a light and illuminating a marbled floor. He stepped back into the hallway to let Lauren enter, then followed her inside, shutting the door and locking it behind them. He took a step forward, noting the kitchen to his left, at the same time that Lauren said, "Royce," and whirled around and right into him.

He closed his arms around her, righting her footing. "Easy, sweetheart. Big guys like me take up a lot of space." He swiped a strand of hair from her eyes, fighting the rush of desire. "What were you going to say?"

"Kiss me," she said, and pressed up on her toes and melted her mouth against his.

His will to resist this woman, to make sure she was inside her apartment safely, and then leave, faded with the touch of their lips, damn near crumbling into ash when he felt her tongue press past his teeth. A low growl escaped his lips as he deepened the kiss, his hands sliding around her back to mold her closer. There was innocence in the kiss, sexuality undiscovered, a trait so rare, so raw, so intimately just for him, that he knew nothing but need. Possessive, hot need.

Before Royce knew what he was doing, he had her pinned against the wall, his legs trapping hers, his body molding her close. He deepened the kiss, drinking her in, craving more of her, wanting more of her. And when she whimpered, there was no right or wrong. There was only the moment, the woman, the…cold gust of air coming from his right. He stilled, his ears registering the too evident sound of car horns coming from the street level.

Royce tore his mouth from hers, his breathing ragged, hers as well. "Is your window open, Lauren?"

Another loud horn sounded and she stiffened, her eyes going wide. "I never leave my window open." Her brows dipped. "Is it broken?"

He pulled her into the kitchen. "Stay right here to be safe and let me check it out."

She nodded. "Yes. Okay." He started to turn and she grabbed his arm. "Be careful. I have a fire escape. It would be easy to crawl into my window." She let him go and reached for her purse. "I'll have my phone in hand in case there's trouble."

Royce was already rounding the corner by the time she finished the statement, making sure he was out of her sight when he pulled the gun from under his pant leg. He eased into the darkness of what appeared to be a living room, a fireplace in the center of the wall directly in front of him which was framed by windows, one of which was open, a curtain fluttering wildly around it. No obvious sign of forced entry, but that didn't mean anything.

He flipped on a light, taking in the huge, overstuffed blue couch and matching chairs with plush cushions that would be far too easy to turn into a bed. The image of slipping Lauren's naked body beneath his on that very couch sent a wave of pure heat through his loins, his cock thickening uncomfortably against his zipper. Royce scrubbed his face and loosened his tie. Holy hell, he was in big trouble when he was holding a gun, and thinking of turning a living room into a bedroom, instead of who he might need to shoot with that gun.

With the dining room to his left, Royce could see Lauren staring at him over the bar from the kitchen.

She'd seen his gun so he stopped trying to hide it. He motioned to the only other room, which had to be her bedroom, warning her he was headed to her private space.

He entered the room and flipped on the lights, illuminating the elegant antique furnishings that included a large, too suggestive, sleigh bed. The now familiar scent of vanilla and honey flared in his nostrils, taunting him.

Quickly, he surveyed for an intruder, checking the closet, bathroom, and yes, under that damnable taunting bed. When he returned to the living area, he called out, "All clear," and went to the window, using the curtain to shove it closed, intending to get finger prints later, if he decided the situation merited it.

She appeared at the end of the hallway, her lipstick smudged, her gorgeous green eyes wide with worry. Her gaze lowered to his weapon, then shifted to the curtain he'd pulled shut, dismissing his gun as if it were expected, but then, she worked around law enforcement, so maybe it was expected for her. "Was my window open?"

"It was," he confirmed and shoved his gun back into the holster at his calf. "But nothing's out of order that I can see. Why don't you take a look and be certain?"

She was already scanning and heading to her bedroom. He wanted to follow her, but would not. He stayed by the window and waited until she returned, her shoes gone, and somehow that little detail made his cock twitch. It was as erotic as if she had taken off much more. This woman got to him; she got to him in a bad way.

"Did maintenance have a reason to be in here?" he asked, stopping near the doorway to the bedroom in case she needed him, or so he told himself.

"No," she said returning to the living area, stopping just in front of him. "Well, sometimes they do fire alarm inspections. Maybe it was something like that. But they shouldn't have left it open. I'm calling them tomorrow to tell them so, too."

He smiled. She was such a contradiction. All sweet and shy,

but also feisty as hell.

She cleared her throat. "Um, well. So. I guess we are...safe." She hesitated. "Can I get you something? A drink? Something to eat?"

You. I want *you.* "I should go," he said. "Before we both do something you'll regret tomorrow."

She stared at him a moment, then crossed her arms in front of herself protectively, as he'd seen her do before, withdrawing into herself. "I understand," she said. "Thank you for... everything. And I'm sorry for your truck. And the fact that your picture will probably be in tomorrow's paper."

He knew right then that she thought he didn't want her. If he let her believe that, she'd never let him inside these walls, or hers, ever again. And for reasons he didn't try to understand, reasons that had nothing to do with why he'd sought her out tonight, he couldn't live with that.

"I want you, Lauren," he said, not allowing himself to think about what he was doing, about how she might read his actions when he confessed all to her. There were only the consequences of doing nothing, and those he simply couldn't live with. He stepped forward, closed the distance between them. He slid a hand to her cheek. "You have to know that by now." He bent his head, brushed his lips with hers, a soft caress meant to seal his message, meant to be brief. Her arms uncurled, her hands settling on his chest, the touch searing him with the promise of more. She swayed toward him, her body seeming to melt into his. Suddenly, the brush of his mouth over hers turned to something more passionate, something he'd vowed to leash.

He started to pull back, he meant to pull back, but she moaned, soft and sexy, and he had to have another taste of her just one last taste and then he'd leave. He'd leave, but she'd know he wanted her.

Somehow, he ended that one last kiss several kisses later, and before she could protest, he bent down and scooped her into his arms. This woman wasn't just any woman. She was his duty and... more. She was more. He didn't know why. He didn't need to know why. He simply needed to do what was right. And though stripping her naked and burying himself deep inside her might sound pretty darn right, it wasn't, not now, not tonight. But later. Oh yeah, later, he was going to do that and so much more.

He crossed the room and sat down on the couch, the same one where he'd imagined her naked and beneath him. He settled her back against the arm, with her backside across his lap. Over the thick ridge of his cock he had no hope of hiding.

"We need to talk," he said, brushing ringlets of long auburn brown hair out of her eyes.

She blinked and shifted just enough to press her soft, round bottom a bit more directly against his erection. "Don't do this," she pleaded. "Don't make me think. Don't make me analyze or worry. For once, I just want to escape it all."

He knew that feeling, knew it all too well. And he also knew it was dangerous; it drove exactly what he didn't want. Regret. "Why tonight, Lauren? Why me?"

"I don't want a politician, or someone my father would approve of, or someone who—"

"I get it," he said, cutting her off, stopping the rest of an answer that had come too fast, too easily, when he was tormented by this woman, by what he was feeling, by why her 'be careful' had tightened his chest.

"I'm your rebellion sex, the guy who isn't good enough for you except when you want to get back at your father? Is that the deal here, Lauren?"

Her eyes went wide. "Oh, God, no. That's not what I was saying." She brushed her lips over his. "But that doesn't mean I don't love that you're everything I never allow myself to experience. You're…"

"What?" he asked, feeling a gnawing in his gut. "I'm what?"

"Everything I want to be and I'm afraid I might never be," she whispered softly, her lashes lowering with the confession. Her emotion, and more of that delicate vulnerability she'd shown him earlier, washed over him, softening him. It hit Royce then, just how much trust she'd given him by showing him this side of herself, by declaring her reasons for doing so. Trust he didn't deserve, trust he was certain she would regret. Resolve formed inside him. He was destined to fail her, but that failure wasn't going to be now. He wasn't going to leave her believing she wasn't gorgeous and desirable.

He scooted her off his lap and settled down on the floor in front of her, his hands sliding up Lauren's calves, to her knees that she'd primly pressed together. The heady scent of her perfume, her home, her very feminine presence, seeped into his senses.

She stared down at him, a soft 'doe in headlights' look on her face. "Royce?" His name was a soft plea on her lips, filled with uncertainty. He'd confused her, sent her mixed messages in his effort to do what was right.

He felt like a wolf, a hungry wolf who wanted to devour this woman, and there was no way that didn't show in his eyes, no way the energy, the need he felt for her, didn't radiate off of him.

"You're beautiful," he said, softly, calmly, when the rage of hormones inside him was anything but. He kissed her knees, one and then the other, reaffirming his decision to let her pleasure be his tonight. "And I'm going to show you how much I mean that."

She swallowed hard, her delicate, kissable throat bobbing with the action. "I'm not sure I know what that means."

He brushed her dress up her thighs. "You will," he promised and kissed her delicate little knee again.

She laughed a nervously feminine sound. "I'm not sure I know what that means either."

"You don't need to know what it means," he said, his fingers tracing the lace of her thigh high pantyhose, the sexy lingerie choice confirming what he'd always suspected. Lauren might be prim and proper on the outside, but there was a sensual woman beneath the exterior who wanted to come out and play. He wanted to be the man she played with. He wanted to be that man tonight, but no matter how tempting that might be, tonight wasn't the night. But he'd be damned if he'd allow her to doubt his desire for her, his absolute, complete attraction to her. "You just need to know how it feels." His hands slipped inside her thighs, easing her legs apart, his lips trailing a path up one leg.

She moaned softly as his tongue traced the top of the lace hose and she slipped further back against the sofa. "Royce, I…" His fingers slid over the damp black silk of her panties. She moaned again. "Oh."

He slipped his finger beneath the fabric, the sweet sound of her pleasure spurring a hunger in him for more. He caressed the sensitive, swollen flesh, and explored the slick proof of her arousal. She moaned again and dug her fingers into the cushion, trying to sit up.

"Royce..."

He moved to frame her body with his, his elbows hitting the cushion, his mouth above hers. "I'm going to take you to bed Lauren, but not for the reasons I want to. I'm going to take you to bed and put you *to sleep*."

"What?" she gasped against his lips. "No. I don't want... I—"

He smothered her protest with his mouth, kissing her, deeply, passionately, then promising, "I'm going to put you to bed right after I make you come," he assured her, scooting down her body, his palms caressing her breasts, making her pant. He settled in front of her now closed knees, his fingers finding the lace of her panties under her dress. "You do want to come, don't you?"

"Has any woman ever told you 'no' when you asked them that question?"

He kissed her stomach. "You're the only woman I'm worried about." He used his hands to urge her backside to lift, pleased when she complied. Royce rolled the material down her hips, over her long, sexy legs, tossing the panties aside. He skimmed her calves, returned to her knees, which he found held real appeal for him. "You're beautiful," he said, heat roaring through his veins as he urged her knees apart. "Open for me again, Lauren."

Her lashes lowered and lifted. "I'm..." she let out a breath, "I'm nervous."

Nervous. His chest tightened with the honesty of her admission, at her continued trust in him; he wanted to be worthy of deserving it. Even more so, at the underlining inference that someone had given her a reason to feel embarrassed. He didn't like that. He didn't like it at all. Protectiveness flared inside him and he moved to her, sliding his hand to her face and kissing her. "You have no reason to be nervous with me. Not now, not ever."

"Says you," she whispered.

"Yes," he agreed. "Says me and I hope says you too very soon." He nibbled her lip and then, before she could feel anything but pleased, eased one of her legs over his shoulder and settled into the intimate V of her body.

Royce felt her stiffen, heard her gasp as he ran his tongue over her swollen nub and then drew it between his lips, suckling her gently. His fingers stroked her slick, wet folds, teasing and pleasing, until he slipped one, then another inside her until she was squirming against him, rocking with the movement of his hand and his mouth. Until she cried out and he felt the muscles of her body clench around him, felt his cock throb with the burn to be inside her. Until he licked and soothed her to a soft sigh and her muscles relaxed.

When she finally stilled completely, he kissed her stomach, only to find her covering her face with her hand. She wrapped her arms around him and buried her face in his neck. He eased her back to look at him.

She was embarrassed. Nervous and now embarrassed. He hoped he met the guy that had messed with her confidence one day. Oh yeah, he did. "You have no idea how sexy you are, do you?" he asked, nuzzling her neck, his hand stroking up her back.

"Royce," she whispered, refusing to look at him, and he wasn't going to force her, wasn't going to push her. But he knew now, more than ever, that had he given her no reason to believe he wanted her, she would have pushed him away. She would have built a wall he would have never been able to climb.

Royce scooped her up and carried her toward the only bedroom he'd seen when inspecting the house. The room was dark, but Royce ignored the switch, his eyes adjusting quickly. She needed the shelter of the shadows, and he wasn't going to take that from her. Not now, not this evening.

A fluffy white down comforter sat on top of the mattress and Royce settled them both down on top of it. When she tried to curl into him, to press her body to his, he ran his hand over her hair, kissed her, and then gently turned her back to his front. "Sleep, Lauren," he murmured.

She tried to turn, looking at him over her shoulder. "But—"

He kissed her. "I'm not going anywhere."

She seemed to consider arguing, but slowly turned back into his arms, softening into the crook of his body, the tension sliding away from her. "You aren't what I expected, Royce Walker," she whispered and almost instantly her breathing settled into a slow, steady rhythm, which told him just how influenced by the alcohol she'd really been.

He nuzzled her cheek, drew in the scent of her, and knew he was in big trouble. He didn't snuggle, he didn't linger with women, and he damn sure didn't get personally involved. Not for years, not since a youthful near marriage that had been so wrong, in so many ways. He'd wanted a career in the FBI. She'd wanted him home, focused on her. The breakup had been bad, and truth be told, she'd been right. He'd been more dedicated to the agency than to her. His duty to his country, to the agency, had left no room for a woman, not one he called his own. But he wasn't in the agency anymore, and at thirty-four years old, he was no longer a young college kid who hadn't lived and learned. And Lauren affected him like no other woman ever had. And he saw no way around her hating him in the morning.

"You aren't what I expected either, Lauren Reynolds," he whispered.

CHAPTER
FOUR

Lauren woke without opening her eyes, the aches in her body sending her a warning. Slowly, she forced her lids to lift. "Oh," she moaned, hand going to her forehead. It was pathetic that the tiny amount of alcohol she'd consumed the night before had given her a hangover.

Shifting, hoping a new position would ease the pain growing in her head, she froze, memories of falling asleep in Royce's arms flooding her mind. The realization that she was alone slammed into her like a concrete wall. "I'm such a fool," she whispered. Of course he was gone. Of course he'd left without even a word. She'd all but thrown herself on him, and good gosh, she must have made a fool of herself, because he hadn't even taken full advantage of her willing state.

She pressed herself to a sitting position, an action that made her lightheaded, but the true pain was her humiliation. Royce Walker had given her a pity orgasm. If that wasn't the most embarrassing thing in the world, then what was?

Her brows dipped, her nostrils flaring with an unexpected scent. Coffee. She smelled coffee. How could she smell coffee? Was this some odd, hangover trick of her senses? And then it hit her. Royce. Royce was here and he'd made coffee. A mixture of relief, pleasure, and then panic washed over her. Her gaze went to the barely cracked doorway. He was out there. Royce was in her living room. Oh good gosh, how was she going to face that man knowing she had all but begged him to have his wicked way with her? Life had suddenly taken a path to full frontal embarrassment.

She looked down and realized she was still wearing her dress from the night before. She swallowed hard. And she had no panties on. They were out there, in the living room, with Royce, the man who'd taken them off of her. She pressed her hand to her face. She had to do something, had to change clothes. Yes. Change clothes.

Lauren shoved aside the blanket covering her, fighting the throb of her head, and rushed to her closet. She quickly tugged her favorite long red silk robe off the hook inside the door and slipped it over her dress. It wasn't much, but it was extra coverage, extra armor. She cringed. How was putting on a silk robe which amounted to a piece of lingerie helping her situation? She tore the robe off and threw it to the ground. She didn't want to look bedroom ready and a robe was bedroom ready.

She was about to head to the door when her gaze caught on her image in the mirror above her dresser, and she quickly brushed fingers through the wild mass of her hair. Her mascara was smudged, her lipstick gone, her general appearance that of someone who'd drank too much and slept too little. She fought the urge to go fix her face, not wanting to seem too affected by this man, like she'd primped for him, even though she wanted to.

She shook herself, told herself to calm the heck down.

Maybe the scent of coffee was her imagination, a post drinking, post orgasm, morning after fantasy that she'd conjured from a deep craving for a caffeine IV. Or maybe Julie had come by to get the gossip on Royce. Julie! Yes! She had a key. Julie was here, not Royce.

She laughed at herself, ignoring the disappointment in her stomach, and rushed to the bedroom door but still didn't yank it open. Instead, she eased into a position where she could peek outside, scanning the empty living room through the crack, and bringing the dining area into focus. And that was when her breath lodged in her throat.

Royce was sitting at the kitchen table, looking quite comfortable and at home while laughing at something he was reading in the paper. His jacket and tie were gone, a few buttons on his shirt were undone, and he'd rolled his sleeves up to display his powerful forearms, one of which flexed as he raised his coffee cup to his too full, too sensual mouth. The one that had done so many wonderful things to her, that she wanted him to do again.

Without warning, he lowered the paper, and smiled at her. "Good morning, Lauren."

She cringed at the realization that she'd just been busted staring at him. Could she ever stop making a fool of herself with this man? She pulled open the door and forced the breath she'd been holding to trickle from her lips. "I didn't think you'd still be here."

"A gentleman never leaves a woman in need," he said playfully, suggestively.

In need. Lauren felt her cheeks heat. She'd made a fool of herself and she had to amend that and amend it now. "I'm not."

He lifted his cup and chuckled, a deep, masculine, sexy sound that made her stomach flip flop. "I'm talking about caffeine and aspirin."

He stood up and held out a chair. "Come join me and I'll get you both."

***

Royce studied Lauren where she lingered in her doorway, unmoving, rumpled and sexy as hell, trepidation pouring off of her. But there was interest in her eyes, attraction in the air between them that morning had done nothing to dissolve. And Royce knew that no matter how many excuses he'd given himself for why he'd stayed: the open window that made no sense, the assignment from her father, the egg and the champagne that had come with a sense of menace he was here for her; he'd simply been unable to force himself to leave. Lauren intrigued him, enticed him, and in short, took his breath away.

"I hope you don't mind that I helped myself to your coffee pot." he said, when the silence stretched onward.

As if his words had somehow released her from a spell, she let out a breath, and her entire body seemed to ease with the act. "Yes. I mean no. You made coffee which makes you my new best friend right about now."

Pleased with that answer, Royce headed to the kitchen to snag her a mug. He returned to find her seated at the table in the chair across from the one he'd occupied. Her head rested on one of her hands, elbow on the table, the other massaging her temple.

He placed a Snoopy mug that he'd found in her cabinet in

front of her, and sat down next to her, rather than in his prior seat. He shook the bottle of pills in his hand and drew her attention. "I dug around and found these in your spare bathroom cabinet." He dumped two aspirins in his palm and held them out for her to take.

Surprise etched her features as she searched his face and then reached for the medicine. "Thank you," she said, cutting her gaze to the vanilla creamer he'd swiped from the fridge. She poured some in her cup and downed the pills with the hot, sweet mixture.

"You're uncomfortable with me being here."

Her gaze jerked to his. "No. No. My head hurts and..." She stopped and stared into her cup, palms now wrapping around it. "And I...you know." Her lashes lifted and she seemed to be lost for words, something he was sure the well-known dynamo prosecutor rarely struggled with.

"Tell me," he prompted.

"Oh well, heck. I'll just say it. I'm a little embarrassed about last night. I wasn't exactly proper."

Still honest, minus the alcohol. He'd expected her to be more guarded, expected maybe everything would change with morning light, that she wouldn't be near as enticing as he'd thought the night before. But she was just as refreshingly different from what he'd expected from her today as she had been yesterday. And he knew part of what made her so appealing to him was how real she was. Perhaps the most real thing to touch his life in a very long time. He didn't want her to feel embarrassed. Hell, he'd wanted her just as much or maybe more than she had him. Seeing her so excited had made him burn for more. Her trust meant more to him than acting on that desire.

"Come here." He turned his chair and held out his hand in invitation. She looked at him, nervousness in her eyes. He drew her hand into his, tugged gently, and softly added, "Please."

For a moment, he thought she would refuse, but satisfaction warmed him as she pushed from her chair and came to him. It took so little for her to make him want, to make him need. Such a simple gesture of her willingly sliding into his lap wasn't so simple for Lauren, though. The effort he knew it took for her to reach beyond her inhibitions magnified its meaning a hundred times over.

Before she could change her mind, he wrapped his arms around her waist. "You have no reason to be embarrassed with me. I loved last night."

"But we didn't—"

"I *loved* last night," he repeated. "And since it's the weekend, I would love it if you would spend the day with me."

Her eyes went wide. "You want to spend the day with me?"

He nodded as he laced his fingers behind her neck and pulled her lips to his in a quick but hungry kiss. "What do you say?"

She hesitated. "This isn't exactly how I had this planned."

"Thought you could use me for a night of hot sex and be done with me, huh?"

Her cheeks flushed. "No," she said. "I mean yes. I mean..." She groaned.

He laughed. "Spend the day with me, Lauren."

"Royce." Her voice hinted at uneasiness. "I'm..." She let her voice trail off, then gave a delicate little laugh. "See what you do to me? It's not normal for me to not finish sentences. You're very—"

"Unexpected," he filled in, using her words from the night before.

Her features softened. "Yes. You are very unexpected and I just really don't know how to react to you."

"Honestly." he said. "Just say, and do, whatever feels right."

She considered him a moment, then shook her head. "This is crazy, Royce. I'm *so* not your type."

He wasn't sure he wanted to know the answer but he asked anyway, "And what exactly is my type?"

"Julie," she said. "Blonde and gorgeous and curvy, and—"

He kissed her, his tongue sliding into her mouth, tasting her slowly, with delicate sensuality. "*You* are my type. *You*, Lauren." His knuckles caressed her cheek. "Spend the day with me."

"You want to?"

"Very much."

She leaned back and searched his face, then glanced at the clock above the bar. "Even if I agree, it's ten-thirty. I promised to join my family for lunch at twelve-thirty."

"Then have dinner with me." She hesitated, and he added, "Trying to cut and run on me?"

Her gaze latched onto his, narrowed. "What time for dinner?"

He smiled with his success. "Seven."

"Seven-thirty," she countered, and somehow he knew it was because he'd pressed her into challenge mode, into courtroom battle mode, with his 'cut and run' comment. And he liked the contrast of sweet and spicy that was this woman, liked it so much. Too much.

He shook his head and laughed. "Seven-thirty," he agreed, setting her on her feet before he carried her to her bedroom and forgot dinner altogether. "I'll drop you by your parents' house and save you the cab money if you like."

"You don't have to do that."

"I want to," he said. And he wanted to do so much more with her as well, which was why he set her on her feet, away from him, firmly maintaining his seat. "You should go shower and get ready. I'll be here waiting."

She blinked down at him and he saw the immediate indignation on her face. When her arms crossed in front of her, he knew he was in big trouble. "You have a very bossy way about you, Royce Walker, you do know that, right?"

"So I've been told on a few random occasions," he admitted, trying not to laugh because, damn, this woman was going to put him in his place ten times over. And considering the rush of heat flooding his body, thickening his cock, and setting his imagination into overdrive, he was pretty sure he was going to like every second of it. "I promise to try and tame that part of my personality, but this time, I'll plead my case, counselor. I had your best interests in mind."

"Really?" she asked, arching a brow, and pressed her hands to her hips, opening her body language and letting him know he was winning her over. "How exactly is that?"

He forced himself to stay seated and not reach for her, but it wasn't easy, not at all. That imagination of his was kicking into high gear, and his zipper was stretching right along with it. "Because you see, every second that you stand there looking good enough to eat, I contemplate the many reasons why I should join you for that shower. In which case, I can assure you that you won't make that lunch."

Her eyes went wide, her mouth forming a silent "O" before

she quickly turned and rushed toward the bedroom, her cute, heart-shaped butt demanding his attention with every step she took.

***

Lauren couldn't believe Royce Walker was sitting in her living room watching Sports Center, with her panties somewhere in the general area of his feet, she imagined. But he was, and they were, and well, at least she could face that fact feeling somewhat put together. She'd showered and dressed in black pinstriped pants, a black sweater, and sleek high-heeled boots, which beat the dress from the night before to face her embarrassment by a long shot.

Royce rose from the couch and quickly hit the remote, the dark stubble on his jaw somehow adding to his raw masculinity, if that was even possible. His gaze skimmed over her, taking her in with hot, hungry eyes that had her feeling pretty hot herself. "You look terrific."

"Thank you," she said, unable to stop the heat to her cheeks she normally wouldn't have experienced. It wasn't like men weren't everywhere in her world, using compliments and sometimes insults, to try and persuade her to help whatever their cause might be. But Royce was different, he was...just different.

They were just stepping into her hallway, about to depart, when her phone rang on her kitchen wall. She frowned, knowing this wasn't going to be a call she wanted. No one had her home number. She didn't even know why she bothered with a house phone when her cell was what she lived by. Except her father, who resisted technology, and still favored land lines. Hoping it was him calling to cancel lunch, she rushed inside the door. By the third ring, she brought the receiver to her ear, only to be greeted by the sound of a clock ticking. Her stomach lurched at the familiar sound, the one she'd hoped to avoid when she took the call.

Feeling Royce's comforting hands settle on her shoulders, she blew her hair out of her eyes and replaced the receiver on the cradle.

"Problem?" he asked, stepping so close that his body framed hers, his nearness, his touch, sending a shiver of awareness racing down her spine.

She turned to face him, the warmth of his body radiating into hers. "No, not really. I've just been getting these weird calls. Probably kids being silly. Or someone angry over one of my cases. It comes with the job."

Royce leaned a broad shoulder on the wall beside her. "What do you mean weird?"

"It sounds like a clock is ticking, and then the line goes dead."

"Huh," he said. "And how long exactly have you been getting these calls?"

"Maybe two weeks, and really, they don't bother me. Well," she hesitated, "maybe a little. I've been…"

"Been what?"

"I don't know," she said as she gnawed her bottom lip. "Nothing."

He studied her a moment, and she worried he was going to press her, kicking herself for saying anything, but all he asked was, "Is your number listed?"

She shook her head. "No. And it's a house phone. Who even calls on a house phone anymore? I don't even know why I have one. Maybe the calls aren't even for me. Really, they can't even be about one of my cases. No one could get the number to start with."

"So this is the only line you've gotten them on?"

"So far."

"So far?" he asked. "What aren't you telling me?"

She pursed her lips, kicking herself yet again for the verbal misstep. What was she supposed to say anyway? That the phone calls would seem silly if she didn't have this weird sense of things going on around her that she didn't know about yet? Or that she felt uneasy, like she was being watched? That would make her sound like some wimpy, crazy female, and she wasn't, nor did she want to be treated like one. Her job, her life, had taught her to stay guarded, taught her not to show weakness, and yet, she was failing miserably at just those things with Royce.

She pushed off the wall. "We should go." He didn't move. "Change your number on Monday, and don't forget to call maintenance about that window."

"Okay now, Royce Walker. First you ordered me to shower."

Amusement danced in his eyes. "For your protection, if you remember correctly."

Her stomach fluttered, heat pooling low in her stomach, at the memory of him suggesting he might join her. "And now you order me to change my number."

Seriousness bled into his handsome face. "Also for your protection." He straightened, towering over her, the fingers of one of his hands slipping between hers. "Please. Change the number and call maintenance."

Please. He'd said please. And when he said it with sincerity radiating from those gorgeous blue eyes, he was irresistible.

Again, he'd shown her the unexpected. She didn't think this man had 'please' in him. She liked that he did that he'd said it for her. A slow smile slid onto her lips. "Since you put it that way."

But in the back of her mind, she knew she'd agreed for more reasons than simply Royce's request. Something deep and dark was bothering her. She *wanted* to change her number, she wanted to call maintenance. And a big, macho male, who happened to rock her world and make her feel safe, wasn't such a bad addition to her day, or to her plans for dinner.

FIVE

A few minutes later, Lauren settled into Royce's truck and watched him pull into traffic. "We're going to drive right by my home office," he said. "So if you don't mind, I'd like to swing by and grab something." He glanced at the clock on the dash. "And if you think I have time, I'd like to snag a quick shower."

"In your office?"

"My office is in the same building as my apartment."

"Wow. I'm jealous your office is in your home. I'd never be able to do that with my job."

"When my brothers and I decided to open Walker Security, we bought a small building. We live on the upper level and work on the bottom floor."

"Really? You live with your brothers?"

"A little too close for comfort sometimes," he said with a laugh. "But thankfully, each apartment has its own door."

Lauren studied his profile, watching him maneuver through traffic with the kind of finesse he seemed to have with everything he did. "Oh," she said. "That's a unique living arrangement."

He shot her a quick grin. "Yeah, well, you'll see firsthand

soon enough."

She grinned back at him. "I'm looking forward to it. Families always have great little tidbits to share about each other."

He laughed. "Yes, well, I see we'll need to make this a quick trip. The last thing I need is my tidbits getting out before I'm ready."

Before he was ready, as if he thought he might be ready someday, as if they were developing a relationship.

"So," he said. "I guess I should come clean and tell you that after reading the morning paper, I now know that I'm a close friend of the opposing counsel on your upcoming case. And that I apparently look angry in all photos taken of me."

She cringed. "I didn't even look at the paper. I'm so used to that stuff I tune it out. I'm sorry."

"I wasn't fishing for an apology. I just wanted you to know I am friends with Mark. But we don't discuss his cases and we actually haven't talked at all in a few weeks."

"Thank you for telling me that," she said, meaning it. She liked that Royce didn't have a political agenda; she liked it a lot. "And since I know Mark pretty well myself, I know he's ethical. I know he wouldn't talk to you about the case."

"No, he wouldn't. But I read up on it this morning. Sounds like a pretty sticky case. Let me get this straight. The defendant killed her husband and you're after the death penalty. Mark's defense is Battered Women's Syndrome." He whistled. "That has to be a tough one for you to handle."

She hesitated. "I can't discuss anything that we aren't making public and even that has to be on a limited basis."

"Fair enough."

"You're right," she said. "It's hard. Half of the media is making me out to be the monster here, mostly because the family of the suspect is doing so much of it themselves, especially the brother. But I don't go after a death penalty verdict lightly, Royce. There's a life insurance policy, a big one. And this woman didn't kill her husband in the heat of the moment. She slowly, methodically poisoned him. There were no calls to the police, no reports of violence from this woman prior to the murder. No history of violence anywhere in this man's life at all."

"I read all of that in the paper," he said. "And what baffles me is that Mark runs his own firm and he doesn't take cases for money or fame. He's about justice and right and wrong. He must know something you don't know."

"She's convinced him she's innocent," Lauren said, her stomach knotting. "I don't doubt that. But I don't doubt the woman's guilt either. And damn it, someone has to fight for the man she killed, because he can't do it himself." She waved her hand dismissively, unease tightening her stomach. "Enough about my work. I'd rather talk about you. Tell me about your brothers before I'm in the center of the Walker pack. I know a little about Luke since, I'm sure you know, he and Julie dated, or had a fling, or whatever it was. I never quite figured it out."

He snapped his fingers. "Just like that, we're changing subjects?"

"Exactly," she said with a firm nod. "I was surprised to hear Luke left the SEALs. Julie thought he'd be in for his career."

"He was afraid Blake and I would kill each other if he didn't referee."

"Really? Why is that?"

He cleared his throat. "Blake thinks I order him around too much."

Lauren laughed. "I have a hard time believing that. Blake must be exaggerating."

He chuckled, a deep, sexy rumble that sent a wave of awareness rushing over her, and suddenly they were joking back and forth, and the stress of her upcoming case faded. With every word spoken, every smile exchanged, she found herself more drawn to Royce. By the time they pulled into a rented parking spot outside of his four-story, white brick building, Lauren was feeling as if she were talking with an old friend, surprisingly at ease.

As he held the door open for her and she exited the vehicle, a cool breeze danced through her hair, lifting it, a signal that winter wasn't quite gone yet. She took a deep breath, allowing the lingering season to conjure emotions both past and present. She glanced at Royce as he stepped to her side, wondering where he fit into those feelings.

She followed him into his building, sneaking covert looks at him, wondering how any man could look so good, so ruggedly handsome in a wrinkled suit with a one day beard. But he did look good, oh, how he did. He looked about as perfect as a man could look.

They rode the elevator several floors up, and when she finally stepped into his private apartment, she was pleasantly surprised at what she found. She wasn't sure what she had expected, but it wasn't what she saw. That seemed to be the theme for all things she had discovered about Royce Walker. She found herself standing inside a cozy, warm home, rather than a typical, cold and unfeeling bachelor pad, with a kitchen to her left and a bar that opened to a large living space that said Walker Security was doing well, because this was Manhattan, where space and quality came with a price tag. The decor was definitely masculine, warm hues of brown and tan, and free of female frills, with overstuffed chairs and a large couch. And of course, an oversized, manly flat screen television with large floor-to-ceiling windows on either side.

Standing just inside the doorway, Royce tossed his keys on the counter that divided the living area from the kitchen.

"Make yourself at home," he said with a smile. "I'll shower and change, and then we can be off again."

Lauren nodded, eager to explore. "Take your time."

Royce started to turn, but stopped, reaching for Lauren and pulling her into his arms. His mouth found hers for a quick kiss. "You can be nosy if you like."

She grinned. "I plan on it."

He laughed and started down the hall. Lauren's gaze followed him, admiring his ogle-worthy backside until he disappeared into what she assumed was a bathroom or bedroom. For a moment, she simply scanned the room. She was standing in Royce Walker's apartment. Who would have ever thought it could happen? Surely not her. The too hot, too sexy, Royce Walker who'd given her an amazing orgasm the night before. That was surely something to smile about, and so she did, slowly walking into the living room and stopping to look at various pictures sitting on tables and hanging on walls.

There were several photos of his brothers. At least she assumed that was who the two men in the shots were, judging from their resemblance to Royce. Then there was a picture of an older couple with enough of the same resemblance to him to have her guessing they were his parents.

"Hmm," she murmured under her breath. She would never have thought Royce was so sentimental or family oriented. All his bad-boy charisma appeared to hide something deeper.

Interesting.

Settling down on the couch, she continued to survey her surroundings. The fireplace was massive, taking up half a wall to her left, and inviting images of cold, winter days snuggling with Royce in front of warm flames. Nice, she thought. Of course she wouldn't be around to find out, so she wasn't sure why she was even contemplating such a scenario.

Sighing, she wondered how she went from having her one and only one night stand with a bad boy, to being with Mr. Virtue, Mr. Dangerously Appealing and destined to break her heart. She grabbed a box of photos on the table and lost herself in what was a history of the family the Walker family. How long she sat there she didn't know, but a knock on the door made her straighten. "Royce, it's Luke. Open up."

Surely, she should let Luke in, and admittedly, she was curious to meet the brother who had seduced her best friend and perhaps broken her unbreakable heart. She rushed toward the door, only to have another knock sound before she could get across the room. Impatience was evidently a Walker family trait. Opening the door, her eyes went wide at the handsome man before her. A girl could get overwhelmed surrounded by so much testosterone. It appeared good looks also ran in the family. As in the proverbial tall, dark, and handsome storybook men.

Before her stood a man much like Royce, but not Royce at all. He was smaller, not that the man was small, because he wasn't. Next to Royce, small was actually pretty darn big, and Luke was well over six feet tall, impressively broad and muscular, with brown eyes and short hair he'd retained from his days as a Navy SEAL.

His brows dipped at the sight of her. "Who are you?"

"You Walker men have a way with words, don't you?"

Luke frowned and then burst out laughing. "Sometimes we speak before we think."

Planting her hands on her hips, she added, "And not nicely, I might add." She stepped back from the door to let him enter.

As soon as the door closed behind him, Luke turned to Lauren and held out his hand. "Luke Walker. Can we start again?"

"Funny how your brother had to 'start again' as well." She smiled, and offered him her hand. "Lauren Reynolds."

"You're—"

Knowing what was next, Lauren pulled her hand free. "Please don't." She hated being referred to as "his" daughter. "Yes, my father is Senator Reynolds." She gave him her back, retreating toward the couch.

Luke laughed. "I was actually going to say you're Julie's best friend."

Lauren stopped walking. There was really no way out of her stupid misstep. She was a bit too defensive about her father. And how interesting that Luke commented about Julie, when she'd just been inquiring about him the night before.

Turning, Lauren found Luke snatching a cinnamon bun off

a tray on the bar. He leaned on the edge. "Want one?"

He wasn't pushing her over her stupid retort. Instead, he was giving her a reprieve, and she appreciated it. "No. I don't even want to think about food." She paused for a beat, feeling the churn of her stomach. "Ever."

Luke joined her on the couch, sitting at the other end, already on the last bite of his roll. "Did my brother get you drunk and take advantage of you?"

"I certainly did not."

Lauren and Luke turned at the sound of Royce's voice. This was her first time seeing him in casual attire, and he didn't disappoint. Dressed in snug, well-worn jeans and a black T-shirt that hugged every inch of his muscular body, his long hair, freshly washed and loose around his shoulders, there was an edge of lethal wildness barely suppressed, barely contained, that had her wishing she'd worked harder to set it free the night before. "No, he didn't," Lauren agreed. "I seem to bring out the gentleman in him." The words were out before she could stop them, and she felt her face warm with color.

Luke looked at Lauren and then his brother. "What am I missing here?"

Royce cleared his throat. "I need to review a couple of files with you." He paused pointedly. "Downstairs."

Lauren eyed Royce. "I can take a hint. You want to talk to your brother alone. I'll wait here."

Luke arched a brow at Royce. "Doesn't miss a thing, does she?"

"No," Lauren said before Royce could answer. "I don't."

"I'll only be a few minutes," Royce promised.

Lauren nodded and reached for the remote. This was new. The woman waiting on the man who was taking too long to get ready.

***

Royce followed Luke into his apartment. "Blake's in the kitchen," Luke told him, of their other brother.

"When isn't he in someone's kitchen?" Royce mumbled, considering Blake's appetite for both food and revenge against the drug lord that had killed his fiancée were damn near legend.

Royce entered the kitchen and eyed Blake, who was quickly gobbling up junk food, his long hair neatly tied at his nape. "It's a little early for cookies," Royce informed him.

Blake smiled a bright white smile. "It's dessert. I ate leftover pizza first."

Luke grimaced. "That pizza was a week old, man."

Blake shrugged his broad shoulders. "Tasted fine to me."

Royce frowned and looked at the wall clock. "Aren't you supposed to be at the airport by ten?"

Blake glanced at his watch and shoved the chair from the table. "Ah, hell," he said. "I'm late." Then he glared at both his brothers. "I know this airport contract pays us, and pays us well, but I hate these weekend security meetings. Next Saturday, one of you is going."

"They like your ATF background," Royce reminded him.

Blake waved on his way out of the room. "We're talking about next Saturday."

The instant he was gone, Luke turned an expectant look on

his older brother. "Well?"

Royce let out a long breath, and leaned against the counter. "I have a situation."

"A situation?" Luke laughed. "Is that what you're calling a gorgeous woman in your living room these days?" Royce gave him a *go to hell* look. Luke raised his hands in mock surrender. "I'm listening."

"You already know Reynolds asked me for a favor."

"Did it include sleeping with his daughter?"

Royce grunted. "Not exactly."

Luke's eyes widened incredulously. "Not *exactly*? What in the hell does that mean? I was joking."

"Someone's been sending him threatening notes, and Lauren has been mentioned."

"Do they have any idea who might be responsible?"

"No, he doesn't. She doesn't know about any of this and he doesn't want to tell her until I'm certain there's a real threat."

"And that would be why?"

"He *says* it's because he believes she'll blow off the threat. She works for the District Attorney's office. That makes a person immune to fear in ways most wouldn't be. I'd like to believe him, and after spending time with her, I certainly think his concern is merited."

Luke grabbed a chair, and sat down at the table. "But?"

"I don't know," Royce said. "Maybe he's being blackmailed for something he thinks she won't forgive him for. Which, in and of itself, has bad news written all over it. Then there is an entirely different realm of low to consider, the senator's political motives. He's trying to get Lauren to run for office and she isn't buying the idea. I hate to think he's selfish enough to keep her in the dark over a threat out of fear of turning her 'no' into a 'hell no.'"

"The blackmail angle makes more sense, but then politicians have never made a lick of sense to me, period." Luke's lips thinned. "Tell me you didn't agree to keep Lauren in the dark about this."

"I agreed to check things out," Royce admitted reluctantly.

"Without telling her."

"He pulled out his trump card," Royce explained. "Saving Dad. I figured that merited me doing a quick investigation. I planned on getting in and out."

Luke arched a brow. "I see that's working out well for you considering Lauren is now in your apartment on obviously friendly terms."

Royce flipped a chair, straddling it, his arms on the back. "I planned to feel her out, see if the senator had any merit for believing she'd refuse protection if it was necessary. The rest just…happened."

"You don't let things just *happen* any more than I do. If you have feelings for Lauren, and really, even if you don't, you're headed for deep, muddy waters. I don't care what the senator says, you'd better come clean and do it right now."

Royce slid his hand over his hair. "Yeah, I know. Believe me, I know. But if I tell her what's going on, she'll kick me to the curb in no uncertain terms. If she's really in danger then I won't be able to protect her. I'm…"

"Screwed," Luke offered helpfully.

Royce exhaled and nodded, then explaining the phone call

situation to Luke before adding, "That about sums it up. I'm screwed. I don't see how I can tell her anything until I find out what's behind the letters and the phone calls. And at this point, I've already written my death wish with Lauren. I don't plan to let someone else write hers. She's spooked and she's not telling me why. When I know she's safe, I'll step onto the plank, tell the truth, and wait for her to push me over the edge."

Luke studied him a long moment. "Well hell. I guess I'm going out on the plank with you. Give me a quick rundown of the facts and tell me what you want me to do."

"We have the blackmail possibility," he said.

"Which is a logical consideration."

"But Lauren's not only in a role to make enemies, she's working a death penalty case right now that's getting a lot of attention."

"Yeah, I know," Luke said. "I've read about it in the paper."

"Then you know how much attention the case is getting."

"If this was about her case, why send the letters to the senator?"

"Scare the father into protecting the daughter," he said. "Get her off the case."

"And the calls?"

"Scare her into listening to him."

"I like the blackmail angle better," Luke said. "I assume you've sent the letters to your buddy at the FBI lab?"

"Yesterday," he said, pushing to his feet. "And I'm hoping he can give me something to make this fast and easy to put to rest. But I don't want to count on that and have it not happen."

"Understood," Luke said, standing with him. "I'll get out my magnifying glass and start looking, with a little extra attention on the senator's personal activities. And I'll get surveillance on her office, home, and likewise for the senator, while I'm at it."

Royce gave him a sharp, approving nod, before he headed back to his apartment and inched his way closer to the end of that plank.

CHAPTER
SIX

Royce found Lauren sitting on his living room floor with photo albums spread around her. She turned to face him, smiling. "Oh my God, for a guy, you have so many pictures."

Royce wasn't sure how to take that. "For a guy?" He moved toward her, sitting down after shuffling a couple of albums to the side.

Her smile widened. "Maybe you're not the 'bad boy' your reputation says you are." And then before he could ask about that comment, she pointed to a picture of him hugging his dog when he was a kid. "And you love animals."

He squatted down beside her and looked at the picture, grinning at the sight of his Golden Retriever wearing a pointed hat. "That was Scooter's second birthday."

Lauren giggled, pointing at the picture. "You mean you made the cake for the dog?"

"My mom did, but I asked her to. Scooter was my best friend." He frowned. "He got really sick after eating that cake. My mom later informed me the bone was for him and the cake was for us."

Lauren almost choked, laughter bubbling from her throat.

"How much did he eat?"

His frown deepened at the memory. "The whole thing."

Lauren tumbled over to her side in a laughing fit. Royce watched her, and any other time, he would have laughed right along with her. But every second he was with Lauren, he wanted another, and another.

He liked her, and damn it, he was taking advantage of her, hiding things from her for her father's benefit. She thought he was a nice guy when he was nothing but a lying bastard. And God, what a bastard he was. She was making him crazy. She was adorable right now, and adorable had never been so sexy. He was hard as a rock, ready to rip her clothes off and make love to her. That he knew she'd blow off her lunch and let him only made the temptation all the greater.

He moved toward her, where she lay on her back, and lowered his body over hers, resting his arms on either side of her head. Lauren stopped laughing, suddenly serious. She stared up at him, her eyes simmering with expectancy. And trust. She kept giving him her trust and it tore at him. It tore at him because he wanted to deserve it, and right now, he didn't.

"Don't kid yourself, Lauren. I'm no good guy."

Confusion flashed in her eyes, but only for a moment. "I'll decide that on my own, but thank you anyway."

"I'm not."

"Innocent until proven guilty."

And he would be. He'd be guilty in the end of deceiving her. There was no way around it. The words were like ice water, dousing him with hard reality, and he pulled her to her feet. "I better get you to that lunch before you find the picture of my bulldog 'Rocky' dressed as a clown."

She laughed. "You're not serious."

He sighed. "There's a reason I wasn't allowed into the K9 unit."

And when she smiled at him, he knew he'd do just about anything to keep those smiles coming his way. He just wasn't sure 'anything' would be enough.

***

Lauren stepped into her father's house feeling more than a little out of sorts. This thing, whatever it was, between her and Royce, was confusing. Of course visiting her father's place always made her uneasy.

Voices led her to the dining room where she found not only her father and stepmother, but to her surprise and discomfort, her stepbrother, Brad Foster. She wouldn't have come had she known he'd be here. Everything about Brad sat wrong with her, from his personality to his mousy brown hair, black rimmed glasses, and standard uniform of a pressed button-down shirt and a blazer. Brad looked up and smiled at her. It took tremendous energy for her to smile back. "I thought you were out of town, Brad." Lauren entered the room as she spoke, a slight edge to her voice she couldn't seem to contain.

"I flew in late last night," he said, his eyes following her movements.

She hated the way Brad watched her all the time. "It was too bad you couldn't make it to the party."

"Morning, Lauren," her father said, settling his napkin in his lap and reaching for a crystal glass filled with iced tea.

"Morning, Daddy," she said, and then forced her attention

to her stepmother, "Hello, Sharon."

Lauren sat down at her place setting, directly across from Brad, flipping her napkin open. The table was filled with an array of brunch items. Lean cuts of roast beef, croissants, fresh fruit, and potato salad. "I'm starving. The food looks good." Despite the rather nauseating company, her stomach was feeling better, as was her head.

With a wink, her father smiled. "Well then, by all means, let's eat."

"Brad was just telling us about his most recent case," Sharon commented, clearly aiming to take some sort of jab at Lauren. She always had an agenda.

Brad leaned back in his chair, arrogance etched in his chiseled features. Lauren couldn't help making a hasty comparison between Brad and Royce. Although Royce was arrogant, he wasn't a snob. Royce was confident. Brad oozed an "I'm *better than you*" cockiness that drove her bonkers. "Just a little corporate trademark case," Brad gloated with fake humbleness. "A few million in jeopardy. Nothing as exciting as the murder and mayhem Lauren favors."

Lauren was reaching for her glass when Brad's words hit her. Her hand froze around the chilled drink. Slowly, she withdrew her hand, fixing Brad with a frosty stare.

A slow, poisonous smile turned up the corners of her mouth. "I protect the public. Do you have a problem with putting criminals behind bars?"

"I don't think it's appropriate for a senator's daughter," he commented dryly.

Her mouth dropped open for a moment, then, through clenched teeth, she demanded, "And how exactly does your trademark war you're litigating better serve the public than putting a murderer behind bars?"

"I guess I don't consider putting a battered woman in the electric chair justice for the public or anyone else."

"You don't know anything about this case," she said, barely containing the urge to reach for her drink again and throw it in his face.

"Brad, I think that's enough," the senator chided.

"Yes, enough, Brad," Sharon added, but there was a hint of satisfaction in her voice.

Lauren almost snorted. Of course it was enough. Her father had spoken. No way would Sharon have said a word until he did.

"What is it with your dislike for law enforcement, Brad?" And she couldn't help taking a jab. "You have some skeleton in your closet you don't want discovered?"

Brad flung his napkin on the table. "Now just one damn minute."

"Enough," Sharon said more firmly this time.

Lauren and Brad stared at each other, and she made sure he saw the contempt she felt in her eyes. After several seconds, she pushed to her feet. "I'm not so hungry after all." Lauren headed to the kitchen, filled a cup with coffee and headed to the den, her favorite room in the house, where she fully intended to try and calm down while waiting for the cab she was about to call.

She entered the room of warm browns and heavy oak, lined with law books she'd spent hours of her life studying. It was an escape for her, a place of peace after her mother's death.

Setting her coffee down on the nearby desk, she turned to the books, eager to make a selection relevant to her upcoming trial, and temporarily forgetting her cab. She stood there, lost in the text, as she had so many times before. That was, until a faint thickness in the air made the hair on the back of her neck stand up. She turned, finding Brad far too close for comfort, a mere foot away, at most. It was unnerving. She hadn't heard him approach. She stiffened, knowing how aggressive he could get. He took a step closer, and she had nowhere to go but into the bookshelf.

His eyes traveled a slow path up and down her body, and then settled on her face. "You know, I've always thought you were quite beautiful when you're angry. Sometimes I get you fired up just to watch the way your eyes sparkle when your temper flares." He stepped closer and reached to touch her cheek.

Lauren turned her head to avoid his touch. "Don't," she bit out.

He pulled his hand away, but his eyes felt like a melting ember on her skin. "We'd be good together, you and I."

"Brad, stop," Lauren said, looking at him, wanting him to see the distaste in her eyes.

"You're afraid of how it would look," he said, his hand going to the bookcase beside her, trapping her in a corner. "But you shouldn't be. We aren't blood relatives. You lost your mother. You found me. The press will eat it up. We'll be everyone's love story."

She shut the book. "You're talking craziness, Brad."

His hand slid to her cheek and she slapped it away. Panic rushed over her. He never touched her and that he did now set off warning bells. She tried to step around him. He moved with her, blocking her.

"What's gotten into you?" she demanded, hands pressed hard

against his chest.

A wicked grin filled his face as his head dipped toward her. "You have, and I'd like to get into you."

She'd always thought he was a little off somehow, always thought him a little too like some of the unsavory types she put behind bars, but he'd taken it to a whole new level today. She inhaled slowly, more than a little experienced with dealing with people like Brad. "I'm going to give you three seconds to move out of my way before I bring my knee to your crotch and make sure you know it's there. One. Two. Three." He moved, laughing evilly.

She yanked her phone from her purse, even as she walked towards the dining room to tell her father she was feeling sick. Of course, Sharon made a snide remark about 'too much champagne will do that to you' but Lauren let it ride. She just wanted out of the house, out of *this house*. And sadly, she wasn't sure that wasn't exactly what Brad, and Sharon, wanted. Lauren was the intruder, the outsider. She couldn't complain and have it do any good. Her father wanted Sharon and he wouldn't risk losing her; she'd learned that the hard way too many times to count. But ironically, neither could Sharon and Brad quite get rid of Lauren. And for the first time ever, Lauren felt done with this battle, done fighting for her home, for a family that wasn't a family at all. In fact, she was so done with this that she wondered if maybe she shouldn't just let Brad and Sharon get what they really want. Maybe Lauren should just go away and stay away.

CHAPTER
SEVEN

I t was seven-thirty on the dot and Lauren sat at her kitchen table, her laptop open. A thunderous knock sounded on her front door, and a smile tugged at Lauren's lips despite her nervousness over seeing Royce again. There was simply no doubt that he was her visitor, as there seemed to be nothing that man did in a small way.

With a combination of trepidation and eager anticipation, Lauren stood up and ran her hands over her light blue, long-sleeved dress where it tapered at her waist. Her gaze dropped to ensure her skirt rested properly just above her knees, then to inspect her strappy black sandals, somehow comforted to see everything was where it should be.

She inhaled a deep, calming breath and then walked to the door and, without giving herself time to think, opened it. "Hi," she said, her throat going dry even before she took in the sight he made standing there, somehow closer than she'd expected, while appearing bigger than she remembered. His hair was loose around his shoulders, black slacks molding a powerful lower body, his black button-down sculpting a stellar chest and arms.

"Hi," he said, gifting her with a sexy grin that all but had her melting into her tiled floor. "You look amazing, Lauren." His voice was velvety soft and full of welcome male appreciation.

"Thank you," she said, her own voice a bit hoarser than it should have been, but then, it wasn't often a girl had a man like this at her door, ready to take her to dinner while looking like he wanted to eat *her for* dinner. She stepped back into the hallway. "Come in."

A moment later the door was closed, and they stood toe-to-toe, the scent of him, spicy and male, wrapping around her, teasing her senses. Delicately, she cleared her throat. "I should get my purse."

"It can wait," he said, his hands settling around her, pulling her close. "I've been thinking about kissing you all afternoon." He nuzzled her neck. "So, can I?" His lips brushed her ear. "Can I kiss you, Lauren?"

Her hands settled on his shoulders and she laughed softly, surprised yet again by this man. She didn't remember Roger, or any of the other men she'd dated for that matter, ever making her smile this much. They darn sure didn't make her warm all over like Royce did. "You're asking? After last night?"

With an easy step, he managed to back her against the wall, spreading his legs and pinning her with his body. "Last night was driven by champagne and emotion. Tonight is just about you and me." His eyes were hot, his voice warm, gentle. He leaned toward her, intending to kiss her, and she couldn't wait. She lifted up on her tiptoes to meet him halfway, but he didn't let her have his mouth. He pulled back just enough to tease her with what might have been, what she hoped would be, and asked, "Is that a yes?"

Lauren responded by reaching for his mouth with hers again.

This time he didn't stop her. At first he didn't move, and for the briefest of moments, she felt nervous about her actions. But she'd come this far last night, tonight. No way was she backing down now. Instead, she pressed into him, wrapped her arms around his neck and ran her tongue across his bottom lip in a sensual move that, to her delight, made him moan.

Suddenly, he was devouring her mouth, kissing her as if he were trying to possess her. And God, she wanted to be possessed. Her hands went to his waist, and she tried to pull him closer, but he wouldn't move. He nipped her bottom lip and pressed his cheek to hers. "Dinner first," he said and this time, he sounded hoarse, his voice raspy with desire. "Then…we'll talk."

She jerked back and he laughed. "You have a real thing about talking, don't you?"

He kissed her. "Get your purse and let's go eat. Wait. I mean, please go get your purse so we can eat." He grinned. "I did say I'd work on the bossy thing."

She laughed. "Yes. You did. And good thing you added that 'please'." She turned on her heels, and headed to the bedroom, thinking that she might let Royce give her an order or two under the right circumstances, under the most pleasurable of circumstances. She smiled and snatched her purse, heading back to where Royce waited, looking forward to both dinner and what came after dinner in a way she hadn't looked forward to anything in a very long time.

***

Thirty minutes later, with her arm linked with Royce's, Lauren walked into the door of "Eden" and stopped at the hostess' booth. Her gaze traveled the dimly lit restaurant, decorated in rich green colors with plants running around high ledges that lent to the tropical-island ambiance that Royce said he couldn't wait for her to try.

"It's such a cool place," she murmured after he put their name on a list.

"I thought you'd like it," he said, but before he could continue they were greeted robustly by a friendly thirty-something couple, with a baby on the way, who not only obviously knew all three of the Walker brothers well, they owned the restaurant. With energetic, friendly conversation surrounding her, and Royce frequently touching her, Lauren felt a new kind of warmth fill her. She was realizing the significance of his actions. He'd brought her to a place that was so clearly a part of his life, after he'd taken her to his apartment and invited her to be nosy.

"Let me get you two a table," Shannon, the wife, a pretty, petite brunette, every bit of eight months pregnant, said before she grabbed two menus and motioned for them to follow her.

"Don't let Royce get out of line, Lauren," John, Shannon's husband a tall blond who looked more lethal weapon than the lethal chef she'd been assured he was, warned. "Bust his chops freely. You have my permission."

Lauren laughed and exchanged a look with Royce who quickly explained, "I call him 'Shannon whooped.' He doesn't like it."

Shannon rubbed her belly. "Oh, he likes it."

Lauren laughed again, pretty sure her cheeks were going to hurt if this night continued as it was, something that normally only Julie and a rare girls' night out could do for her.

Shannon led them down a hall to a private dining area and circular booth, waving them forward. "Our VIP seats." Once they were seated, Shannon placed the menus on the table. "Enjoy."

Lauren reached for her menu, when Shannon's gaze caught on her wrist. "What a gorgeous watch."

"Oh," Lauren said, wondering why she'd worn the darn thing. "Thank you. A gift from my father." And that recognition of her father she'd just delivered, was probably why he gave her the flashy diamond studded piece of jewelry, she thought. The gift, the many gifts, weren't about her at all. They were about making himself feel, and look, like he cared, even if his actions said otherwise. A point driven home today quite clearly. She'd left his house obviously upset, claiming to be sick, and he hadn't even called to check on her.

Royce's hand slid to her leg under the table, and her gaze met his. Her chest tightened at the understanding in his expression, at the awareness that somehow she'd let emotion seep into her reply to Shannon in a way she normally would not, and he'd noticed. The sincere concern she saw in his eyes touched her, while the contrast it held to the insincerity of her father's gift clawed at her.

"Well it's spectacular," Shannon said wistfully and glanced at Royce. "Give me one of those as a gift and we'll talk about me working at Walker Security."

Royce chuckled. "None of those in my arsenal, but I have a desk and sturdy chair with your name all over them."

She snorted. "You really don't know the way to a girl's gun, I can promise you that."

A waitress appeared with a bottle of wine. "From John," the

woman said, and set two glasses in front of Royce and Lauren.

"I'll leave you two to enjoy," Shannon said and smiled at Lauren. "Nice to meet you, Lauren. Maybe next time we can chat more."

A few minutes later, Lauren and Royce sipped a rich, sweet red wine, each having ordered a pasta dish. "What was all that about Shannon's gun and your desk and chair?" Lauren asked.

"The restaurant is really John's baby. Shannon's an FBI agent I used to work with, and a damn good one, at that. We'd be lucky to get her for Walker Security. And it would be a safer job for her too, which is why John wants her to leave the agency. I can control what jobs she gets and watch her back. And I can make sure the job doesn't destroy her family. The Agency won't do that."

"Do you ever regret leaving the Agency?" she asked, sipping her wine.

"Not once in two years," he said, but she didn't miss the sudden flex of his jaw muscle or the tightness of his voice. "I had some bad stuff go down at the Agency and by the time it passed, I was one foot out the door." He sighed and tapped his fingers on the table, as if drumming out tension. "Right about the time I was contemplating leaving the agency, Blake lost his fiancée in an undercover ATF mission. He was ready to go vigilante and there's no good in that. I needed something to distract him, a way to keep him under thumb, and Walker Security was born. Truth be told, I suspect Blake's walk through hell was the real reason Luke went civilian. Otherwise, I think he would have been career Navy, like our father was career Army."

"Did they ever catch the person who killed Blake's fiancée?"

"No," he said. "That particular Mexican drug cartel leader is still alive and well, and deep underground, but not ever out of Blake's mind. If he finds him, he'll go after him. I never kid myself about that."

She studied him a moment. "And you and Luke will be there with him."

He gave a sharp nod. "Making sure he doesn't end up dead or in a jail cell for taking the guy out."

Heaviness settled in her chest. "And your father?"

"What a lifetime of combat couldn't do, cancer did. We buried him three Christmases ago. My mother lives in Jersey and is thrilled to have her boys nearby. She was yet another reason Walker Security made sense."

"I was a teenager when breast cancer took my mother," she said, emotion thickening her voice. "Seventeen when my father married Sharon."

He didn't say he was sorry or 'oh how horrible' like most people and she knew why. He knew it didn't help; he knew from experience that 'I'm sorry' sometimes managed to open a raw nerve. "And Sharon has been like the Energizer Bunny. She just keeps on staying."

She smiled. "The evil Energizer Bunny."

John appeared at the table with a cordless phone in his hand. "There's a call for Lauren." Her gaze went to Royce's, her stomach suddenly rejecting the few bites of bread and the wine she'd just enjoyed. "No one knows I'm here. I didn't even know where we were going before we got here."

John arched a brow and covered the receiver. "Muffled voice, and car horns in the background. Sounds like a payphone to me."

She sighed. "It's probably a reporter." She reached for the

phone. "They'll just keep calling if I don't take it."

John handed her the receiver and she immediately put it to her ear. "Hello, this is Lauren."

The sound of a clock ticking echoed through the line for a mere few seconds, before a dial tone replaced it, and Lauren felt a chill race down her spine. Her hand began to tremble. These feelings she'd been having of being watched weren't her imagination, nor were the calls pranks. Which meant someone had watched her tonight, followed her to Eden.

Royce reached for the phone, and Lauren let him take it from her hand, barely aware of him listening to the dial tone or disposing of it, until his hand slid to her face. "Tell me what just happened."

She wet her lips. "The clo..." She swallowed the dryness in her throat, her hand going to his wrist. "Ticking clock."

He studied her several long seconds, then pressed his forehead to hers. "You're okay. We'll take care of this. I'll take care of it." He leaned back and looked at her, trailing his fingers down her cheek. "Give me a second." He pulled his phone from his pocket and dialed, then snagged the cordless and looked through the call log.

"I'm at Eden with Lauren," he said into his cell. "She just got a call we need traced." He read off the number and then barely a second later, said, "That's what I thought." He hung up. "Payphone, but Luke's headed over there to check it out anyway." She opened her mouth to protest and he cut her off, "Don't even think about telling me he doesn't have to. He wants to and so do I."

"Is this when you tell me to call the police?" she asked.

"If I did, would you?"

She shook her head. "No. It would end up all over the papers and I can't deal with that, Royce. Not on top of everything else and not when that might be exactly what this person wants."

"Who are you trying to convince?" he asked. "You? Or me?"

"I don't think I have the reasoning skills right now to convince anyone of anything, which makes me wonder if that isn't the idea. Someone wants to rattle me before the trial."

"We could make a list of what this person's motivations might be," he said. "And of all the things I'd put on that list, you picked the one that makes you feel better, the one that makes you feel like you aren't in danger."

"Are you saying you think I am?"

"I'm saying that refusing to accept that you might be is a danger in and of itself. You know that. Your job has allowed you to see what people are capable of."

"You aren't making me feel better."

His hand moved down her hair. "I'd rather make you feel safe." He brushed his lips over hers. "Let's get out of here."

***

Half an hour later, Lauren stood at the door of her apartment, Royce by her side. He leaned in and kissed her. "Let me check it out before you go in."

"I'm feeling pretty good about the bodyguard routine right now," she said. "Feel free." She pressed her key into his palm and then watched while, instead of entering, he felt around her doorjamb.

She squeezed her eyes shut and leaned against the wall, knowing all too well that he was looking for some sort of trip wire or surveillance equipment. It was overkill, she told herself, suspicion and caution built into his blood by a lifetime in law enforcement that he was incapable of fighting. But deep down, caution felt right, and that meant something was very wrong.

The minute he opened the door, his gaze dropped, he squatted then stood, having retrieved an envelope. "Does your doorman allow people to just come and go?"

Lauren stepped toward him, reaching for it. She half expected him to resist. "No. You've seen how he hovers." To her dismay, her hands shook, yet again, as she fumbled with the seal and opened the envelope. Inside she found a single sheet of paper that appeared to be a calendar.

"Today's date is marked off," Royce observed from over her shoulder. "Any idea what it means?"

She shook her head. "No. Should I be touching it? What about evidence?"

"There won't be any," he said, as if he were sure.

Her heart hammered in her chest as she let him take the piece of paper from her hands. The envelope slipped out of her hands onto the ground.

Drawn to Royce's strength, she studied his profile as he examined the calendar. His jaw was tense, his eyes probing and intense. He bent down and picked up the dropped envelope, inserting the page back inside.

When he spoke, his voice was unaffected. He seemed calm and collected, so very unlike her right now. "I need to check out the rest of the apartment." He reached out and smoothed a piece of wild hair behind her ear. "Stay put."

It wasn't a question, and though taking orders normally wasn't her cup of tea, it suited her just fine if it meant she didn't have to go inside alone. She nodded and leaned against the wall, suddenly feeling exhausted. The adrenaline high from her initial scare was wearing off to be replaced with stark fear.

***

Royce waited to pull out his gun until he stepped inside the door. He didn't want to upset Lauren any further, and right now, things that wouldn't normally bother her, might. She was just that rattled, and that sensitive.

He searched the apartment, all the while aware of the leaden feeling in his gut. Gathering his thoughts, he stood in the bedroom, giving himself a minute before returning to Lauren's side. He wasn't sure what weighed on him more heavily, Lauren's safety or the fact that he knew she didn't give trust or control easily, but she was giving it to him. No, the thing that weighed the most heavily was knowing he was bound to hide the secret pact with her father until this blew over. Part of him even wondered if he could simply never tell her, but he discarded the idea, knowing all too well that he'd end up captive to her father, and even more so, to guilt. Running a hand through his hair, he let out a loud breath. Then he heard Lauren's voice. "Royce?"

He holstered his weapon before responding. Walking into the living room, he found her looking nervously around the room. "Woman," he said, "I thought I told you to wait."

She bristled. "You took forever. I was worried."

He smiled, unable to help himself. The idea of her worrying about him wasn't such a bad one. "You were, huh?"

Her brows knitted together. "Why are you smiling?"

In several long strides, he closed the distance between them, wrapping his arms around her waist, and pulling her close. "Because I'm not used to anyone worrying about me. I'm not leaving you tonight. You do know that, right?"

"Promise?"

"Promise. I need to make some phone calls and talk to the doorman, though. You do whatever you do at night, and I'll finish up as soon as possible."

**

An hour later, Royce sat at Lauren's kitchen table, and ended a final call with Luke, having confirmed the phone booth was in Time Square, and had been swept for fingerprints. He pushed to his feet, more than eager to join Lauren in the living room where she'd snuggled under a blanket in a red silk robe to watch a True Crime show. He'd tried to convince her to change to something else, but she'd refused.

Royce rounded the couch to find her fingers curled under her chin, her eyes shut, her breathing heavy. He smiled. He wasn't sure he'd ever been so good at putting a woman to sleep. But the adrenaline rush from the fear, on top of limited sleep the night before, had clearly worked a number on her. And never before had he found himself just watching someone sleep, so lost in taking in every delicate line and curve of someone's features. He shook himself and bent down to kiss her, stroking his hand over her fiery hair.

He flipped off the television, kicked off his boots, and slid onto the couch behind her. She sighed and snuggled that perfect round backside of hers to his front, and dug deeper into her pillow. Royce smiled into her hair and made a silent vow. If he was going to be forced to keep a secret from Lauren to keep her safe, then he damn sure was going to make whoever was messing with her feel the pain he was going to.

***

Dirt Diver sat with his booted feet kicked up on the wooden surface of a cookie-cutter hotel desktop, a smile on his lips. The monitor in front of him displayed an image of Royce Walker acting like a watchdog to Lauren Reynolds, camped out by her couch as she slept. He snorted. Royce Walker and the Walker brothers. Like they could stop him from getting to her. Like anyone could stop him from getting to her. He liked that the brothers were bad asses by most people's standards, his included. He liked it a lot. That meant Lauren would feel protected, safe, secure. That meant that when he reached inside her world and sliced it to bloody hell, she'd feel as gutted as she'd made him feel. As she'd made so many people before him feel. That meant she would know just how lethal he was, just how ready he was, just how good he was. The bitch would know his name before this was over. Oh yeah, she'd know his name and she'd know why he'd come for her. No one, not even Royce Walker and his piece of shit brothers, were going to protect her.

CHAPTER
EIGHT

Lauren woke to the phone ringing. Blinking, she eased up on her elbow, realizing she was still on the couch and the light streaming through her blinds said it was already Sunday morning. She glanced down to find the blanket from her bed on top of her. Any pleasure at knowing Royce had done something so thoughtful, so intimate, faded with the incessant ringing demanding her attention.

Behind her, she heard the phone lift, her *home phone*, and reality hit her. It was her caller again, her...stalker. She hated that word but that's what this was starting to feel like. She sat up straight, her breath lodged in her throat. The next few seconds felt like eternity, as she waited to see what would happen, but there was only silence, until Royce hung up the receiver. Almost instantly, as if he'd already had someone on the line, he spoke into his cell phone, or so she assumed, "Yeah I know," he said in a low voice. "Too short to trace. And yeah, whoever it is has to know I'm here since they knew she was with me last night. And yeah, I know what that means." He ended the call without a goodbye. She sensed rather than heard him heading in her direction.

Lauren's fingers curled into the blanket as she waited for him to join her. "I woke you up," he said, rounding the couch to sit down next to her. "Sorry about that."

"I heard the phone ring," she said, turning to him, aware of him as a man despite her distress, aware of how their legs melded together, of his smell, spicy and male, both arousing and comforting. "And I heard you say that whoever the caller was knows that you're here and 'yeah you know what that means'. What does that mean?"

"I should have stepped into the hall," he said. "You didn't need to hear that.

"Yes, I did. I don't want to be coddled, Royce. I want to know what I'm dealing with."

He considered her a moment, and then nodded. "Fair enough. No coddling." He reached up and brushed hair from her eyes. "The call was a taunt that was, in my professional opinion, and Luke's as well, meant to tell us that whoever this is believes that he, or she, is untouchable. But you know from your job, as well as I know, that they all think that they're different than the other guys. That they really aren't un*touchable*. You know that."

"You really don't think this is just someone trying to scare me, do you?" she asked, knowing she'd pressed him about this before, but unable to stop herself from doing so again.

"You can ask me that same question framed every which way you can think of and it's always going to be the same," he said. "I think it's better to be safe than sorry. And you have experience and good instincts or you wouldn't be good at your job. No matter what I say, you know what you feel. Don't ignore a gut feeling. I learned that the hard way a very long time ago. So I'll ask you now and probably again, what do you feel?"

"I don't rattle easily, and I wouldn't have slept if you hadn't stayed with me. That's not me. I see a lot of nastiness and I've learned to compartmentalize it outside my job."

"You have to," he said. "Believe me, I know. And I'm here." He slid his hand under her hair, around her neck, "And not just because of these threats. I'm here because I want to be." He leaned in and brushed his lips over hers, and a shiver of pure need slid down her spine.

"I'm glad you are," she whispered, unsure what was happening to her, between them. She'd never felt so consumed by a man's presence, so completely drawn to him.

He ran his hand down her hair. "I might have woken you up but I do have morning gifts."

She laughed. "Morning gifts? Hmmm. Please tell me its toothpaste because I shouldn't have just kissed you."

"Better," he assured her. "I called the corner deli and they delivered donuts."

"You had donuts delivered and I didn't hear the door but I heard the phone? Now I'm questioning my survival instincts."

"I was smart enough to step in the hallway to make the call and then have the doorman text me when he was bringing them up. I wanted to ask him a few questions anyway, so I made it worth his while. Cash and donuts buys a lot of information. A little trick an ex-cop taught me."

She laughed, liking that he shared those insider jokes with her, but somehow didn't seem a part of the insiders at all.

He pushed to his feet. "Stay put and I'll bring them to you."

Lauren smiled as he headed to the kitchen, and wondered if he even realized when he gave orders. Somehow, she didn't think so, and was odd considering what she knew of herself and her dislike for bossy people, she found it endearing rather than irritating. And this wasn't an order she intended to follow. She threw off the blanket and rushed toward the bedroom and her bathroom.

Not five minutes later, Lauren had brushed her teeth and hair, and washed her face, before returning to find Royce sitting on the couch with donuts and coffee for them both laid out on the coffee table.

"A girl could get used to a big brawny man attending to her caffeine needs every morning," she said, joining him and sitting down beside him again. She reached for the coffee mug and inhaled. "The only thing better than caffeine in the morning is sugar."

"I couldn't agree more," he said. "And you just happen to live down the road from one of the best donut makers in the city."

"I'll be the judge of that," she said, opening the bag and pulling out one of a chocolate glazed variety, to take a bite. "Hmmm. Okay. Pretty darn good."

He leaned in and kissed her, licking his lip afterwards. "You had icing on your mouth."

Lauren felt her cheeks heat, and pretty much, her entire body, too.

"I'm staying the rest of the weekend."

"What?" She asked in surprise at the announcement and

then immediately set her donut on a napkin he'd placed on the table and shook her head in rejection. "You don't have to play bodyguard, Royce. The building is secure."

"And yet you wouldn't have slept if I hadn't been here last night. I'm staying with you or you're staying with me. I'd rather stay here so I can evaluate what is going on with these threats in your environment and whether they are likely to continue. But," he pulled her close, his lips lingering above hers, "I'd welcome the opportunity to have you in my bed."

"Royce," she said, trying to think past the warmth spreading through her body. "You're impossibly—"

"Bossy. Yes. I know. But I'm going to fight you on this one and I'm not going to apologize. I told you to listen to your gut. And my gut tells me to keep you close."

"I don't want you to babysit me, Royce."

"Apparently I've not been clear. You interest me, Lauren Reynolds, like no other woman has in a very long time. I *want* an excuse to stay with you. Now, I just need to hear you say you want me to stay."

She did want him to stay but he confused her, sent her mixed messages. "Where did you sleep last night?"

"I didn't."

"You didn't sleep? Were you that worried about these calls?"

"I dozed off leaning against the couch at some point," he said, dodging the question.

She studied him a long moment, reading between the lines of his many mixed messages. He was worried and he wasn't someone to worry without cause. He thought she was in trouble and no matter what his motivation, his duty, or his interest in her, it mattered to her that he was here for her.

She brushed her hand over her cheek. "You can't stay with me if you're not going to sleep. You have to be exhausted."

"I'm not promising either of us are going to get any sleep."

Heat and nerves collided inside her at those words. She wanted Royce, and yet, she was way over her head with him, inexperienced and vulnerable, two things she didn't like to feel. She was too drawn to this man and it scared her.

"How about we go to my place so I can shower and change and pick up some things?" he asked, continuing. "Then, we can hunker down here and watch a movie, or I can beat you at tic tac toe. I don't care what. Anything that will get your mind off this mess."

"I have work I need to do," she said, "but…yes. Okay. I think it might do me some good to escape a bit."

"Perfect. So let's eat this bag of donuts and you can do whatever women do in the morning to get ready, and we'll take off." He released her and reached for the bag and they turned on the news and chatted. But any relaxation Lauren felt ended quickly as a media clip of her and Royce, rushing from the hotel, flashed on the screen. Then another of the crowd gasping as something was thrown all over them.

Lauren was glad she'd just finished off her donut. She was no longer hungry. "He wants attention," she said, without looking at Royce. "He got it."

"He?"

She glanced at him. "Gut feeling."

"Ah," he said. "Well. It's all over the news. Why not file that police report?"

"Someone throwing alcohol at us is in the news," she said. "My phone calls are not. And you and I both know the police will do less than what you're doing and someone will blab. This kind of thing feeds copycats. I don't need to invite that kind of attention to me, or anyone in a similar position on a tough case."

"Are you confident this is about the case?"

She inhaled and let it out. "I don't know. I have ticking clocks and one day marked off a calendar. How do I know what that means? Logic says it's this case, though. That's all I can go on."

"Do you have your files on your computer? Can you go through them and make a list of the most likely suspects?"

"Royce, you were FBI. Is there even one of the perps you took down that would send you a Christmas card?"

"No," he said. "But I know the ones that were the most vicious and the most likely to lash out. We need to start there."

"I have my files."

"Then when we get back here, we'll go through them. We'll get this behind you. I promise."

Lauren wasn't one to lean on other people, but in that moment, she was secretly far more thankful for that promise than she was willing to admit to anyone, even him. And not because she didn't appreciate his efforts. Because she knew that if she let him know just how rattled she was, if she admitted it to him, she'd have to admit it to herself. The way she compartmentalized the bad stuff that came with her job didn't work that way. There was an order to the way she dealt with things. She had to maintain control. Not Royce.

***

Several hours later, Lauren shivered as she stepped off the elevator and into the corridor outside her apartment. "Well, we didn't beat the rain," she said, shivering from the cold droplets that lingered on her black jeans and red t-shirt, as well as her hair. "I hope the sandwiches we walked two blocks for are worth getting wet over. I've never tried this place."

She scooped her keys from her purse. Royce's cell phone rang and he dropped his overnight bag on the ground, and Lauren took the bag of food from him so he could answer it.

He held his phone and punched the 'answer' button as his gaze dropped to the bottom of the door. He answered the call with, "I'll call you back," then ended the connection and stuck his phone back onto his belt.

Lauren's gaze settled on the envelope on the ground and she knew that had to be what he was reacting to, and she was downright chilled to the bone now. "We've only been gone a few hours. There have to be security cameras."

"There are and they showed no evidence of anyone but us at your door in the past few days. Let me have your keys."

Lauren set the bag on the floor and handed them to him. He took them and checked the door over before opening it and grabbing the envelope. "Stay here."

"Right," she said stiffly. "I've got the drill down. You go. I wait."

He tilted her chin up with his finger. "I'll make this go away, Lauren. I promise."

"Keep saying that," she encouraged, confessing more than she should, more than she told herself just hours before that she would, but unable to stop herself. "It helps to hear it."

***

After Royce searched the apartment, he found Lauren in the hallway and gave her the 'all clear' to come inside. Standing at the kitchen table, he showed her the calendar sheet he'd already pulled from the envelope with an additional day marked off. This time there was a message made from cutout letters.

Lauren frowned, reading it. "The countdown continues." She shook her head. "There's no ending date for me to have any idea where this is headed. It's making me crazy."

"When you see that paper and hear the ticking clock, what's the first thing, or things, that comes to your mind?"

"This case. It's a death penalty case. Well, there is this other..." She pursed her lips. "No. Never mind."

"What?" he asked. "Say it. It's better to look at all options than not."

She leaned one hand on the table. "I hesitate to bring this up because I was second chair, but my first death penalty case, a guy named Sheridan, goes to execution soon."

"When?"

"Ironically, two weeks after this new trial begins but it's been stayed several times. It could easily be again."

"Who was the first chair?"

"He's dead, natural causes."

Royce stiffened at that news. "You're sure it was natural?"

"Not only did the man practically inhale his weight in grease every day, the phrase 'smoke like a chimney' was created in his honor. He had a heart attack. It's a reach, but it's what came to my mind on several occasions, so there it is."

Royce grabbed his phone and punched in Luke's number, before giving his brother the Sheridan execution and case to research. He asked Lauren a couple of questions for Luke and then ended the call.

"I hate that your brothers are being bothered with this," Lauren said, her hands on the back of one of the chairs. "I hate you're being bothered with this. I know you have work of your own to deal with."

"They don't question what I need any more than I question what they need. We have each other's backs." He pulled her against him, her hips to his, his arms around her waist. "And I have yours."

Her hand settled on his chest and he doubted she knew just how much her touch scorched him, how much she affected him without even trying. "You barely know me," she argued.

"But I want to, which means keeping you safe so I get the chance." She shivered and he ran his hands down her arms. "Why don't I start a fire before we eat? I noticed you have wood."

"I'd like that," she said. "I think I'll go throw on some dry clothes." She started to turn and paused. "Thank you."

"You don't have to thank me."

"I do." She hesitated. "Just...I do." She rose up on her toes and pressed her lips to his.

Royce knew she meant to make it a quick kiss and then escape, but she was tiny and soft in his arms and felt more perfect than anyone had in a very long time. It tormented him to know he was deceiving her but he shoved aside the reality he'd eventually have to face and wrapped his fingers around her neck, holding her to him. His tongue pressed into hers, stealing one sweet taste before he murmured, "Hurry back. I'm hungry." And if she wasn't clear that he wasn't talking about sandwiches, she would be soon.

CHAPTER
NINE

Royce watched Lauren disappear into her bedroom, thinking about the senator's insistence that she would dismiss a threat, and put herself in harm's way. Sure, he saw her caution about overreacting, but he couldn't blame her in the role she was in with the DA. Most importantly thought, she wasn't under-reacting either or pretending nothing was wrong. The senator clearly knew something he wasn't saying, something he didn't want Lauren to know.

Royce headed to the front door and unzipped his bag and replaced his wet Yankees t-shirt with a dry white one on his way to the door. He had Luke on the line the instant he was in the hallway. "Senators can't give stays of execution," Royce said. "I get that, but—"

"They can influence them," Luke finished for him. "I'm already on it. I'm trying to find any connection between the senator and the Sheridan case, be it past or present, or both."

"You mean *I'm* trying," came Blake's voice in the background. "And I'm already on it. Apparently, you're taking all the credit."

Luke grimaced at Blake's comment and continued speaking

to Royce. "I've recruited help. While Blake works the Sheridan angle, I'm working on anything and everything the senator has touched in the past year. Are you going to tell him about the phone calls and the calendars Lauren is getting?"

"Not yet," Royce said. "Let's see what we come up with first."

"Exactly my thought," Luke agreed. "This whole secrecy thing just doesn't add up."

"Agreed," Royce said, glancing at the caller ID as his phone beeped. "Speak of the devil, the senator is calling me. Text me when you find something out." He ended the call and flipped over to the next. "This is Royce."

"Update, son. What is happening with my daughter?"

"That's exactly what I'm trying to find out," he said. "And it would be easier if we told her what is going on."

The senator grunted. "Absolutely not."

Royce ran a hand through his hair. "She is going to hate us both when she finds out we didn't tell her."

"Then don't let her find out," he said bitingly. "Where is she now?"

"She's safe."

"Translate that to a detailed assurance."

"I'm with her, out of her hearing range."

"Well done," he said. "I've got to head to a meeting. I'll check in with you tomorrow."

"Have you?" The line went dead.

Royce dropped the phone to stare at it in disbelief. Damn it to hell, he'd hung up. And without one single question about the progress on finding out who was behind the letters or what the lab had found out. More and more, something didn't add up.

***

Lauren returned, having dried her hair, dressed in black sweats, a tee, and slipper socks, to find Royce stoking a fire that seemed to be on its way to a nice blaze.

He rotated on his heels from where he squatted, apparently hearing her approach, his gaze hotter than the fire as it traveled a path up and down her body and settled on her t-shirt. He laughed, a deep rumble from his chest. Damn, she loved his laugh. "Lawyers have more fun?" he asked.

"Julie got it for me since I always tell her blondes have more fun. I told her the shirt proves nothing." She motioned to the kitchen. "I'll grab the drinks. I'm starving."

A few minutes later, they both sat on the floor with their laptops at the ready, their Reubens on plates. The fire crackled and rain splattered against the window.

Lauren took a bite of her sandwich and sighed. "Either it's good or I'm just really, really hungry."

"It's good," he agreed. "I haven't had one of these in a long time." He opened the container with his cheesecake and took a bite. "It's good, too."

"I've never seen anyone eat dessert with their meal instead of after."

"It's better than before, right?"

"I suppose it is," she agreed and found herself considering him a moment. "You know, you really aren't what I expected."

"You said that before, the other night before you fell asleep. This time you're not getting out of an explanation."

"You're just…different."

"Different from other men you've known? From the

politicians you work with?"

"Everyone else around me. I'm surprised you took the state advisor job. It doesn't seem like you to want to deal with the politics of things."

"I tolerate the politics because I'm able to influence decisions that impact the safety of the public. I worked some pretty intense post 9/11 FBI operations. I don't ever want the people of this country, this city, to see 9/11 happen again. And as I suspect you have done, I made the decision to grin and bear what I had to, to make an impact, or at least try. Frankly, I'm shocked you aren't working for your father's law firm."

She took a sip of her drink and set it down. "My father is all about money and power. That's just not who I am. It wasn't who my mother was either. Looking back, I think she chose to be a professor over a practicing lawyer to avoid the differences between her and my father." She opened her cheesecake and took a bite. "Oh, that's good." She shoved her sandwich aside.

"Now look who's eating out of order," he teased.

"I ate half my sandwich," she said. "That's enough for me. You want the other half?"

"I thought you'd never ask," he said and grabbed her plate, setting his now empty one aside. Then he surprised her by asking, "Didn't I read you were engaged at some point?"

Her fork stilled in her mouth a moment before she nodded and set it down, her gaze fixing on the orange flames of the fire. "Yeah. I was."

Royce slid a finger under her chin. "I'm sorry. I didn't mean to pry."

"You're not. It's just not a happy subject."

"He hurt you."

"I caught him in bed with another woman." She held up a hand. "And don't do the sympathy thing. After I was over the initial shock of his betrayal, I was actually relieved." Lauren turned to face him, leaning her elbow on the couch, her legs curled to her side. "I wasn't happy with him. I knew long before we broke up that he didn't want me. He wanted control of my father's law firm. By him taking it, I didn't have to deal with my father's nagging for me to take over."

"He hates it," she said. "And he really hates this case I'm about to go to trial with, because the defendant is playing the battered woman card and I'm being painted as a monster. He's been getting hate mail and phone calls over it."

"Have you seen any of the mail?"

"I don't want to see it. I get plenty of my own. It's part of the job. But that's just it. It's my job, not his. I'm helping victims fight for justice and that feels good. I hope my ex stays with my father's firm forever and the two of them live happily ever after making tons of money. That's not what motivates me."

"Wait. Are you saying he still works there?"

"My ex and my stepbrother are controlling partners."

"I'd have kicked his ass and wiped the floor with him and then thrown his stuff out the door with him. I can't believe your father let him stay."

"It's business."

"It's family."

Her chest tightened. "Not everyone has the kind of bond with their family you seem to have."

He studied her a long moment and then pushed the table away from them. He scooted back to sit beside her, his back against the couch before pulling her legs over his lap. Awareness rushed through her, and something else, something warm and right, like she'd never felt with another man.

"I owe you an apology," he confessed, his hands settling on her legs.

"An apology?" She laughed. "For eating my sandwich? For being bossy by nature? Because I can't imagine what else you have to apologize about at this point in our short relationship."

"I judged you by a stereotype before I met you. I thought you were the pretty, spoiled senator's daughter. And now, more than ever, I not only know how unfair that was, I know how much it eats you alive."

"Thank you," she said, moved by his honesty. "I appreciate that more than you can know, but if you're apologizing for your assumption, then I have to apologize for mine. I thought you were an arrogant ladies' man. Single, good looking, in your thirties, with two different women at the two different functions I saw you at."

His chest expanded with an inhalation before he exhaled. "I haven't been much on serious relationships but I was engaged once, right when I joined the agency. It was the wrong time, the wrong situation, and I was the wrong man for her. I was high on my job, and she wanted me home when I wanted to catch the next bad guy. The deeper and more dangerous my work became, the more I saw the writing on the wall. You put bad guys behind bars, they become your enemies and you become dangerous cargo to the people you love."

"Well, I guess I've proven I'm dangerous cargo," she said, a shiver chasing a path up her spine. "And I guess being alone is a small price for fighting for the innocent."

"You're not alone now," he said softly, brushing his fingers down her cheek, sending a tingle of electricity through her body. "I'm here and no one is going to scare me away."

"Have you met my father?"

He laughed. "Not even your father."

"We'll see about that one."

"Yeah," he said. "We will. I'm not going anywhere unless you make me." He turned to his side to face her. "I know I said this before, but I'm going to say it again. I'm not here because of the threats. If they didn't exist, I'd still be here, if you'd have me. I'm here for you, Lauren. I'm here because there is something about you I can't escape, and I don't even want to try."

The rain pelted against the windows, the fire crackled in the fireplace. Electricity sparked in the air, intimacy thickening with it.

"I'm glad you're here, and not because of the threats." She hesitated. "Okay, maybe I'm a little glad you're here because of the threats. I'm rattled, Royce. I don't know why; it's not like me, but I am. And I wouldn't tell anyone else that, but I am. And I feel like I can tell you that without it becoming everyone else's knowledge."

"You know what I think?" he asked, lowering his head slowly, his breath warm, teasing her with the promise of intimacy. "I think you need something else to think about." His lips touched hers, a soft caress that traveled her nerve endings. Her nipples tightened, and heat pooled low in her belly.

Nerves fluttered in her stomach, with the awareness of where this was going, but his tongue, his hands, his touch, drew her deeper into the fog of desire. She lost herself in the moment, savoring the feel on him, a soft sound of pleasure escaping her lips as his tongue swept against hers. He deepened the contact and she wrapped her arms around his neck. His hand traveled her back, scorching her with heat, melding her closer. She could feel the desire expand between them, consume them, and leave her with only him.

CHAPTER
TEN

Royce pulled Lauren into his lap to straddle him, the V of her body pressing against the thick ridge of his erection. He wanted this woman, wanted her like he had not wanted in a very long time. Wanted in a way like he'd never wanted. Her hair was soft on his face, and that damn vanilla and honey scent was driving him wild. So much of what she had told him had twisted him in knots. Her ex cheating on her explained the insecurity he'd seen in her, the fear of intimacy.

He drank her in, kissing her, making love to her with his tongue, and vowing to be the man who showed her just how sexy she truly was.

"You're beautiful," he murmured against her mouth. "And your ex was a fool."

"Royce, I—"

He swallowed her words, working his hands under her shirt to her soft skin, not allowing her to reject his words, showing her how much he meant them. She reached behind him and tugged loose his hair, twining her fingers into it. Her touch was like silk and fire at the same time, soothing him even as she ignited his hunger. He touched her, filled his hands with her high, full breasts and shoved down her bra to tease her plump nipples.

She shifted on top of him, arching against his cock, and he moaned with the ache and pleasure that crashed into him. He tugged at her shirt. "Take it off."

She leaned back and stared down at him, and he saw vulnerability wash over her face. He wrapped his fingers around her neck and pulled her mouth to his. "You. Are. Beautiful. And I want to feel you next to me." He reached over his head and tugged his shirt off, trying to make her feel more comfortable by undressing first.

Her gaze swept his chest, her teeth sinking into her bottom lip. "You're beautiful," she said, her hands splaying over his pecs, his arms.

He kissed her, hard and fast, caressing her sides, her breasts, before easing her shirt up again. "Take it off. Let me feel you next to me."

She pulled it over her head and tossed it and he cupped her breasts, teasing her nipples even as he unhooked the front clasp of her bra.

Her lashes fluttered, her hands covering his. He rolled her to the ground and eased her legs apart, settling his hips between her legs and going down on top of her.

Their eyes locked and held, the connection, the desire he felt with Lauren, expanding inside him, feeding a possessive need to pleasure her, to protect her, to hold her. He kissed her, trailed lips down her neck, taking his time until he lapped at one perky nipple, and suckled.

The soft sound she made, the twine of her fingers in his hair, worked a number on him. His zipper stretched, his cock throbbing uncomfortably. He lapped at the other nipple, scraped it lightly with his teeth, and then began a downward path to dip his tongue into her belly button, skimming her pants down her legs. He raised to his knees and pulled them off.

He smiled as he traced the dark triangle of hair, dipping his fingers between her thighs, and caressing the silky wet proof of how aroused she was. "No panties?"

She lifted up on her elbows, her cheeks flushed, pleasure etched on her face as he dipped a finger inside her, stroked her. "I don't like panty lines," she murmured.

"I hear ya," he said. "Panty lines are a bitch."

She laughed, her breasts jiggling with the action. Damn, she had nice breasts. High and full with pretty pink nipples. He pulled her sweats off her feet and took her socks with them. And why the hell her pink painted toenails seem to make him hotter and harder, he didn't know. It was just Lauren. Everything about her turned him on.

He leaned in and kissed her clit. "Be right back."

Royce sat up and yanked off his boots, then stood and made quick work of getting rid of the rest of his clothes, but not before he yanked a package of 3 condoms from his pocket.

She stared at it and he knew immediately what she was thinking. "I don't walk around with condoms for easy access." He tore one free from the package, reached down, and pulled her to her feet. "Blake shoved it in my hand as I was leaving the building. He's a smart-ass, but for once I'm glad." He tugged her to her feet. "You don't want the floor. Carpet burn is a bigger bitch than panty lines."

She laughed, and the soft, silky feminine sound was music to his ears. He settled onto the couch with her straddling him, his cock between them. He grabbed the condom. She covered his hand with hers. "Let me." Her other hand wrapped his shaft, tightening around it, and her gaze dropped.

He let go of the package. "As much as I'm a guy who enjoys a woman's attention to his cock, if you keep staring at me like that, I'm going to forget why I need that condom." He wrapped his hand around the back of her head and kissed her. "I need to be inside you."

She tore open the package and glanced up at him before rolling it over his cock. "Now, come here," he said, the instant it was in place. He framed her hips with his hands and lifted her. She guided his cock to the slick heat of her sex, and pressed him inside her.

White-hot burn rushed over him, at the feel of her taking him, sliding down his length and taking all of him. When she'd taken all of him, he fought the urge to move, to thrust, to take.

He kissed her, tasted her, devoured her, inhaled her. She tangled her hands back into his hair, her tongue dancing with his, and he felt her give herself to him. Felt the moment when she forgot everything but this, now, them.

Royce pressed her down against him and then thrust. She gasped into his mouth and arched into him. Slowly, they began to pump until wildness exploded in him, in her. They were moving faster, harder, hands everywhere, anywhere, and he still couldn't get enough of her.

"Lean back, baby," he said, wrapping an arm around her back and flattening his hand on her chest. "I got you." The angle tightened her grip on his shaft and let him see her body, her face. "That's it." He caressed her breast, suckled her nipple, and then thrust hard into her. She moaned and held onto his hand as he began a steady, hard pump in and out of her, watching her breasts bounce, her expression shift with the pleasure, the need.

She gasped and leaned forward, stiffening in his arms a moment before her tight little sex grabbed hold of him and spasmed, milking him right to release. A low hot throb expanded in his cock and then shot his release from his body.

They collapsed together, skin slicked with sweat, her face buried in his neck. Long seconds passed and she didn't move. He knew she was feeling shy, or embarrassed. Damn, he was going to have to fix that. He rolled her to her back on the couch and leaned over her. "I don't know if three condoms are going to be enough. We might need a store run because if you think I even came close to getting enough of you, you're wrong. But for now, I'm going to get rid of this one." He snatched his shirt from the floor. "And because I know you are about to scramble to get dressed, put my shirt on. It's less effort for me to take off of you later." He leaned in and kissed her. "And *that* was an order you won't get an apology for."

***

Lauren awoke naked, on the floor with a comforter underneath her and a heavy arm over her back. She inhaled the spicy male scent of Royce and smiled to herself. She was on her stomach, and she was pretty sure that was because Royce had refused to let her get dressed, so he'd trapped her there.

You need to be as comfortable with you being naked as I am, he'd told her.

I'm very comfortable with you being naked, she'd replied.

Her gaze fixed on the red glow of a fire not tended for a good while. The darkness of the room was lightening, as if the sun was replacing the moon. And unfortunately, as much as she wanted to savor this moment, Mother Nature called.

She tried to inch out from under Royce's arm.

Royce pulled her back against him, rolling them both to their sides. "We aren't ready to get up."

"I have to go to the bathroom."

"Close your eyes and you'll forget."

She laughed. "No. That's not going to happen."

"You're sure?"

"I'm sure."

"Well, damn," he said. "I guess I have to let you up then." He released her and she crawled and grabbed his shirt. He smacked her on the backside and she yelped, drawing a low, sexy chuckle from him.

Lauren stumbled groggily to the bedroom, surprised to see the clock read ten in the morning, until she heard a rumble of thunder. It was still storming. She went to the bathroom and her phone beeped in her purse. Five missed calls from Julie. It rang again in her hand. Lauren shoved down the toilet seat and sat down.

"Yes, my diva darlin'," she said. "I am alive."

"You can't not answer your phone when you have this big case going on and all kinds of public anger. I worry about you."

"Royce is here. I'm fine."

"Rewind. What? He's still there?"

Lauren laughed. "Pretty sure the answer is 'yes'."

"Honey, you know how to make up for lost time and bad exes. I so will not keep you from your play toy but I expect gossip and lots of it. Lunch. We are so going to lunch on Monday."

"Lunch."

They ended the call and Lauren sat there a moment, thinking about how easily she'd said 'Royce is here. I'm fine.' The truth was she was better than fine. Or maybe she wasn't. She pushed to her feet and stared at herself in the mirror.

"Don't fall for him," she murmured. "You can't fall for him." She was vulnerable right now, recovering from the past, and perhaps in danger, and she knew it. She was turning Royce into her knight in shining armor, and she knew all too well that was a fairy tale that didn't exist. She inhaled and let it out. Royce was all man, all sex, and hard masculine beauty. He made her feel sexy and empowered. This had to be about sex and nothing else, or she'd get hurt. She pushed off the sink and nodded, heading toward the living room with one thing on her mind. She was going to have more sex. No. She was going to fuck.

***

Royce was sitting on the couch and watching the news when Lauren returned, stepping in front of him and pulling his shirt over her head. His mouth went dry and his cock stood at attention. "I should remind you we're out of condoms."

"We'll improvise."

She went to her knees and wrapped his cock with her hand. He thickened and pulsed in her palm. She licked the head. "Any complaints so far?"

"You can lick me, suck me, pretty much do whatever you want to me, sweetheart. I'm all yours."

Her gaze met his, a fearless look in her eyes he'd not seen before, that he registered as trouble. Something was going on in her head, and he had to find out what. But she sucked his head into her mouth and he forgot exactly what the problem was. Suddenly, there was only the suction of her mouth on his cock, the drag of her tongue around him, up and down. Her long silky hair teasing his stomach and thighs. The edge of near orgasm, and the final, deep draw of her mouth that took his release from him.

The instant he was off the high of one of the best damn blow jobs of his life, he reached for her and pressed her down onto the couch, settling on top of her.

"What was that?"

"I think they call it—"

"I know what they call it. I want to know what is going on in your mind right now. Why you came out of the bathroom a woman on a mission to give me a blow job."

"I don't know what you're talking about."

"You damn sure do."

"No, I don't."

He slid down her body, and lifted her leg to his shoulder. "Here's how this is going to work. I'm going to take you to the edge of orgasm over and over until you tell me what just happened in that bathroom." He suckled her clit into his mouth.

"Royce... oh... ah..." She rose up on her elbows. "Stop. This is unfair."

He slid two fingers inside her and lifted his head. "You don't want me to stop." He licked her up and down. "Do you?"

"This is torture... oh hmmmm... you're..."

"What was in your head when you came out of the bathroom?" he asked again, swirling her clit with his tongue.

"I... okay." He pumped into her, stroked her. "Ah... okay...

I'll tell you. Just please don't stop and I'll tell you... after." Her head dropped to the cushion. Royce sucked and licked her, his hand covering her breast, teasing her nipple. His finger pumped in her like he planned to do with his cock again, and very soon. And when she spasmed around his fingers, he licked her and lavished her with soft caresses of his tongue until she collapsed, panting from release.

He settled her leg down beside him, and eased up her body. "I really need you inside me right now," she whispered.

"No condom," he said, unable to resist pressing the thick ridge of his erection in the silk heat of her sex. "And you owe me an explanation."

"I'm on the pill, "she said. "So please. Now. I need you."

A strange feeling expanded in his chest with the understanding that she'd been on the pill for her ex, for another man. Something possessive and uncomfortable that he'd never felt before. Something that made him need to feel her, to claim her.

He slid off the couch and took her with him, turning her to face the cushion, and spreading her sex with his fingers to enter her. He drove into her, hard and deep, when he'd never taken the 'pill' explanation from another woman. But she wasn't another woman, and she wasn't like any other woman he'd ever known. He wrapped his arm around her, squeezed her breasts and pressed his lips to her ear.

"What happened when you came out of the bathroom?"

"Nothing," she panted. "I just... wanted you." She gasped as he sped his pace, pumping and thrusting, and twisting her nipple roughly.

She covered his hand with hers, dropped her head against

him. "Oh God. It... you... I'm..." Her tight little sex grabbed a hold of him and squeezed.

He exploded inside her, groaning loudly with the force of it. Shaking until she had all he had to give, every last pump and drop of him.

When finally they were quiet, he didn't let her go. He held her there. "Now, tell me."

She buried her face in her hands. "There's nothing to tell."

He pulled out of her and grabbed his shirt, turning her to face him and giving it to her to dry off. He pressed his hands on the couch on either side of her, framing her body with his. "Talk to me, Lauren."

"I don't know what you want me to say."

"I've told you before. The truth. Say what you feel."

"Confused. I feel confused. You went from one night stand to my private bodyguard."

"You were never a one night stand to me, Lauren. But maybe that's the problem. This has gone way farther than you wanted it to." He started to move away. Damn, this woman had a hold on him that he didn't understand.

She grabbed his arm. "No. No. It's not that. I... I just don't understand what we're doing."

"I thought we were getting to know each other. Apparently, I'm helping you work another man out of your system by way of sex."

"Oh God, no, Royce. No. There isn't anything to work out of my system."

"He hurt you and messed with your head."

"He did. You're right. That doesn't mean I'm using you. It means," she inhaled and let in out, "it means you scare me. If this is just sex then I need it to just be sex. Clearly. Cut and dry. I don't want to mix it in with conversation and pretend fluff to feel better about that."

There it was. The truth. What she really felt, and he was damn glad she'd told him, that she hadn't played games. That she had honesty in her. And what was he doing? Hiding things from her, lying to her. Anything he said to her now, she'd question later and he knew it. But he was in too deep to turn back. If he confessed, she'd kick him out, push him away, and he'd struggle to protect her.

Royce kissed her and then pushed her away to stand up and grab his pants. He stepped into them, and she blinked at him, looking dazed and confused. He yanked the blanket off the floor and crossed back to her, wrapping it around her and squatting in front of her.

"I need you covered before I try to prove to you this isn't just sex. I want you, Lauren. I tried to resist and I was weak, and if you sit there naked I'll be weak all over again. There's something going on between us, and I know it's happening fast, but I'm not sure there's any other way two people as drawn to each other as we are can do things. This is new territory for me. I'm not the stay-the-weekend kind of guy, Lauren, but you have to kick me out if you want me to leave."

"Because you're trying to protect me. You're law enforcement. It's your nature."

Those words punched him in the gut, because he knew they were a preview of what was to come, what she would think when he finally confessed his deal with her father.

"I have a staff," he said. "I have resources. If I felt some obligation to protect you, I could put surveillance on you and you'd never know it." He traced the delicate line of her jaw. "I'm here because I want to be. Because I thought you wanted me to be."

"I do," she whispered. "I do want you to be here."

"Good," he said. "And if keeping our clothes on will prove to you that there's more to this than that, then we will step back and start over slower. I won't lie and say it won't kill me, but I'll happily take the couch if that's what I need to do."

She dropped the sheet and wrapped her arms around him, her soft curves pressed to his chest. "Only if I'm on it with you."

His resistance lasted all of a few seconds before his arm wrapped around her body, his mouth closing down on hers, tasting her, drinking her in like a man weeks without water. And as she moaned into his mouth, as possessiveness he'd never felt for another woman ripped through him, he didn't question the need to make her his. He simply knew she was the one woman he had to have, the one he'd never found until now. The one who was going to hate him before this was over. The one who would rip his heart out. And worst of all he was going to be the bastard who deserved it.

CHAPTER
ELEVEN

Monday morning, after a weekend of pure bliss with Royce, Lauren stood in the kitchen holding a steaming cup of coffee, dressed in a tan fitted skirt and cream silk blouse, ready to start her work week. As much as she'd loved her escape with Royce, she'd bypassed work for movies, conversation, and a lot of unforgettable moments that required no clothing, and now she was behind.

Royce appeared in the archway, his dark hair tied at his nape, his jeans and t-shirt molded to delicious muscles she now knew intimately. "I'm driving you to work," he said.

She should have been irritated about the command, but a few of his bedroom orders flashed in her mind—*harder, faster, lick me*— and her mouth went dry. Lauren set her cup on the kitchen counter. "You don't have to take me to work."

"Yes, I do." He leaned on the archway, his shoulders taking up the entire tiny space.

She studied him, reading what he wasn't saying, and nerves knotted her stomach. "Stop. Stop acting like a watchdog. You're making me uptight. You're making me think about the phone calls and the calendar pages. I can't do my job if I can't think straight."

"You have to think about this, Lauren, and you have to look over your shoulder. And I'll be looking too."

"You can't watch me all day, Royce. And even if you think you can, for how long? We didn't get another call, or another calendar sheet, this weekend. Maybe it's over. Maybe this person got their laughs and moved on. Or maybe you being with me scared them off."

"No. He's not tired. He's not scared. He's trying to get you to let down your guard."

"You don't know that. We don't know anything at all. And you're going to make me crazy."

He closed the distance between them and pulled her into his arms. "Just humor me for a few days and play things safe until I get some answers. I'll drop you off at work and pick you up. That way I have an excuse to take you to dinner," his lips curved, "and have you for dessert."

"Bribery isn't going to make this better."

He laughed. "Bribery, huh?"

She couldn't laugh. She couldn't do anything with the invisible vise tightening on her chest. "I've been working criminal cases for years. I've had threats. I did with those what I told you I do with everything else. Threats, bloody pictures, and random body parts in bags. They are the same to me. I put them in this imaginary place in my mind, a box that I seal and don't open unless I have to. It's how I keep going."

"I know," he said. "If anyone gets that, it's me. If I had any other choice, I wouldn't push you on this. There's something about the way this has all gone down that I don't like. I need you to be on alert, and I need you to be cautious until I figure out why."

"Damn you, Royce. That just made me more on edge. I know to be careful. I'm always careful."

"Curse me if you want," he said. "Yell at me. Just do what I say."

She let out a sigh. "What is it about me and controlling men? I'm drawn to them." She stepped out of his reach. "Drive me if you must." She tried to walk around him and he caught her arm. "Please don't. Not now. And I know I'm probably being unfair but I just feel like everything is spinning out of control. I need some space to figure out where my head is."

His eyes, so blue, so piercing, held hers, his expression unreadable, before he let her go. And God, she was so confused and conflicted, because she hated he let her go, when she'd just told him to.

***

Two hours after arriving to work, Lauren sat behind her simple steel public servant's desk, in her box of an office. She and Royce had barely spoken on the way to her office and that had her just as crazy as everything else. He'd made her put his number and both of his brothers' numbers in her phone, and told her not to leave the building. No kiss goodbye. Just a quick 'I'll call you later and check in.'

The intercom on Lauren's desk buzzed and she jumped, silently cursing her edginess. She punched the button on her phone. "There is a Jonathan Wilkins here to see you," came the familiar gravelly voice of her sixty-something year old assistant, Alice Harper. She cleared her throat and lowered her voice,

"He's very determined."

Of course he was. His sister was about to go on trial for murder. She could only hope this was heading toward a confession. "Send him in." Lauren leaned back in her chair and waited for her visitor but she didn't, and wouldn't, get up. Not with this particular visitor, whom she'd read the file on. She'd learned a long time ago that sitting behind a desk was as good as towering over a man. It proclaimed ownership of the room, it said she wasn't intimated into standing. It worked with the more dominant types.

Her door was open and it took all of sixty seconds for a strikingly large man, one she knew to be thirty-six years old, to appear in the entryway. And true to his military duty, his hair was short, his jaw strong, his expression hard.

"Hello, Ms. Reynolds."

There was something about the way he said her name, the way it came out almost like a threat that set a warning bell ringing in her head. "Please, have a seat, Mr. Wilkins."

For a moment, he stood there, so still, she almost thought he'd frozen in place, turned to stone, before he gave a surprisingly polite, "Thank you," and claimed a visitor's chair.

"I assume this is about your sister," Lauren prodded, eager to get on with this. He was a time bomb she could almost hear ticking.

"I'll cut to the chase," he replied, bypassing a direct answer. "I know what Beverly did was wrong, but don't you think you are being a bit harsh in your quest for the death penalty? I mean the woman was terrorized by her husband."

Lauren leaned back in her chair, carefully schooling her features into an emotionless mask. "Have you talked to your sister's attorney about this?"

He let out a bitter laugh. "Funny. That's exactly what your father asked me."

She cringed at the idea that her father had been dragged into this, but managed to clamp down on an obvious reaction. "My father is a State Senator. He can't do anything to help your sister."

His lips thinned. "So he says." He shrugged. "I guess that means it's all on you."

"Unless you have new evidence to present, Mr. Wilkins, this case is in the jury's hands."

He leaned forward and pressed his hands onto the desk. "I'm Special Forces. I was away on a mission. I'm all she has since our father died last year. She married that bastard when I was in deep combat territory, and instead of taking care of her, he beat the crap out of her. Had I been here, things might have been different. Had I even known what was going on, things would have been different."

"I can see how much this is upsetting you," she said. "And I understand. But a man is dead and buried, Mr. Wilkins, and his family is in pain. They want his side of the story told."

He pushed to his feet, his voice rising with him. "I let her down. She was desperate to survive. Don't you understand her need to end the pure hell she was living? Do you have no heart, Ms. Reynolds?"

Her heart was what made her job both difficult and rewarding. The victim of this crime was dead, but his family painfully lived on. "Look, Mr. Wilkins. I want to help but I need new evidence. Something to clear your sister. Have your sister's attorney call me. I'll talk to him."

He stared down at her, his jaw tight, his breathing a little too fast. "This isn't over," he said in a low, threatening voice, before turning and storming out of her office.

Stunned, Lauren read the threat he intended. She watched him leave, fingertips pressed to the top of her desk. It wasn't until she heard the front lobby door slam that she realized she was holding her breath and her hand was shaking. She exhaled, rattled when she normally wouldn't be. And she knew why. The calls, the calendar sheets. Royce's paranoia over them. All those things were messing with her head and that meant whoever sent them was getting their way, and she didn't want to give them that satisfaction. She had to shake this off.

Her intercom buzzed again and Lauren punched the button. "You okay in there?" Alice asked, concern in her voice.

"Yeah," Lauren said. "I assume he's gone?"

"Oh, he's gone," she said in a disgusted tone. "And he did so quite loudly."

"I heard, but I wanted to be sure."

"I called the building security and alerted them when I heard him raise his voice in your office. And you have a call. Mark Reeves."

Beverly's attorney, and the timing was just too perfect. "Put him through," she ground out through her teeth.

Alice transferred the call, and Lauren answered, and she didn't hold back, nor did she bother with 'hello'. "Sending your client's relatives over here to harass me into giving you a plea deal is not only not cool, it doesn't seem like your style."

"I have no idea what you're talking about. I just got your message, and was returning your call."

"I was returning your call from Friday," she corrected. "And

Jonathan Wilkins just paid me a delightful little visit. One that ended in a threat and a slammed door."

"Ouch, Lauren. I'm sorry. I had nothing to do with that. I talked to him this morning and told him a deal wasn't looking good for Beverly. He wasn't happy."

"No, he wasn't. How about warning me when you have a loose cannon? We might not be on the same team, but we aren't enemies."

"He's Special Ops. I thought he had more control than this. He's just another reason to put this behind us. Let's talk plea bargain and avoid the trial. Save us both a lot of time and headaches."

"Not unless you've changed your last proposal."

"The jury will be sympathetic to a battered woman," he argued.

"You mean a cold blooded killer who meticulously planned her husband's slow death. Poison has precedence in the courts. The death penalty is a strong possibility, and you know it."

"Wouldn't you rather get a sure conviction than risk her walking? I'm good, and you know it. I'm willing to listen to any reasonable deal. Make me an offer."

"First, let me say this, I'm good and you know it." He chuckled into the phone as she added, "That said, you already know my offer, and that's *no* offer."

"And you know that's not reasonable," he argued. "Second degree with an established time period for possible parole. I can guarantee my client will accept if the parole period is reasonable."

"You're joking, right?" she said sharply. "I would never let her see parole. Forget it."

"She's young, a mother of two. Have some heart."

"Life without parole," Lauren countered.

"You can't win a first degree charge and a death penalty sentencing."

She clenched her teeth. "Then what are you worried about? If I overcharge then I'll be the one with regrets. Think Casey Anthony. I am and I know I have the backup they didn't to support my charges. And let me remind you about State vs. Norman. The wife killed her husband in his sleep stating she thought he would kill her when he woke. The Supreme Court said, 'If we allowed this behavior, homicidal self-help'—"

"Would then become a lawful solution and perhaps the easiest and most effective solution to this problem." He paused. "I am well aware of the ruling."

"So you know I'll win," she stated with confidence.

"Juries are a fifty-fifty bet." He sighed. "I can tell we are at a standstill."

"I respect you, Mark. I know you believe in this woman, but you're wrong on this one. I wish you weren't, but you are."

"Let me know if you change your mind," he said. "Otherwise we'll take our chances with the jury."

"I guess we will."

A few seconds later, they said their niceties and ended the call. Her buzzer went off immediately and that was how the next few hours went for her. When Lauren finally managed a breather, she intended to review a file, but instead found herself replaying the moment she'd dropped that sheet and pressed herself against Royce.

"What are you smiling about?"

Lauren's gaze lifted to the doorway, to find Julie standing

there, her simple black suit hugging her voluptuous curves, her long blonde hair resting on her shoulders. "I want details about this weekend."

Lauren glanced at her watch to see if she had lost track of time. "I thought you were going to call me and make sure I could do lunch?"

She shrugged. "Yeah, well, that gave you a chance to say 'no.'"

"It's only eleven o'clock."

"So?" Julie said, claiming the chair Beverly's brother had been in earlier that morning. "It's late enough to qualify as lunchtime."

"I really need to work through lunch. Don't you have any work to do?"

"No morning appointments. I delve into another divorce with the rich and famous again this afternoon. You know Gina Garrett?"

Lauren blinked. "The actress?"

"The one and only. My newest client among quite a few celebrities. Seems I've been named the attorney of choice when discretion is valued."

Laughing, Lauren said, "Yeah, well, you've earned that. You are responsible for divorcing at least half of a professional baseball team."

"And quite discreetly, I might add." They shared a laugh before Julie asked, "Can you at least go downstairs and have coffee with me?"

"I better not," Lauren said reluctantly. A good talk with Julie would be well timed. She hadn't told her about the calls or the calendar pages, because she knew Julie. Julie would call in the

National Guard, but she needed to tell her. She needed her friend, but she was way behind on her trial prep. And then there was her promise to Royce to stay in the building. "Could you grab us some coffee and we can talk here? There's actually a few things I'd rather talk about in private."

Julie's brows dipped. "Everything okay?"

"Not really. No, it's not."

"What did Royce do to you? Tell me now because I swear—"

"He didn't do anything," Lauren said, foreseeing the National Guard call already. "It's not Royce."

Julie studied her a moment. "Okay. I'll go get the coffee, and bring it to you so you can work until I get back."

Giving in, Lauren motioned for Julie to go. "That's good. And yes, I'll be here when you get back, working, unlike some people I know."

"Hey, you choose the type of law you do. I get paid well, and work less."

Lauren rolled her eyes. "So you remind me all too often." She shooed her away. "Go, woman. Get the coffee."

Julie disappeared, and Lauren began taking notes on her case until Alice buzzed her yet again. "Do I really want to know what this is about?" Lauren asked when she punched the button.

"No," Alice said. "Which is why I should just anticipate your response and tell your caller you're busy."

"Who is it?"

"Roger."

What the heck was her ex calling her for? "Tell him I left for lunch." Lauren looked up to find Julie entering her office with two cups of coffee. "And just so you don't have to lie, Alice," she added, "I really am leaving." To heck with staying in the building. She couldn't act like a prisoner and stay sane.

"Consider it handled," Alice said. "And there's a package for you up front."

Probably the psychologist reviews for the upcoming trial. She already knew what it said. "I'll pick it up on my way back from lunch."

Julie's brows dipped. "Now we're going to lunch?"

Lauren pushed to her feet and grabbed her purse with one hand, the coffee with the other. "Yes. Roger just called. Somehow, just hearing his name made me claustrophobic."

"What did that jerk want?" She shook her head.

"Every dime my father is worth," she said. "The same thing he always wants."

***

A few minutes later, Lauren stepped onto the street with Julie by her side, fighting guilt over leaving the building, telling herself this was nuts. She'd had threats before. They wouldn't go away and she just had to lift her head and carry on. In fact, she had to look unruffled or she'd look like an easy target. Royce didn't understand that, and she had to make him.

She chatted with Julie, telling her about her morning confrontation, when an uneasy feeling rushed over her. Damn it, she liked Royce, but he really was messing with her head. Feeling a sudden need to free her hands, she paused at a trash can and tossed her untouched coffee, then slid her purse strap across her shoulder and chest.

"That coffee cost me five bucks," Julie complained. "You didn't touch it."

"It had a bitter taste."

"Oh well, then I'll complain when we go back to your building. Now, talk, girl. Details on Royce and now. If he's as good as he looks, oh baby, I know what kind of weekend you had."

Lauren struggled for a reply, distracted by a sense of being watched. "He's different than other men I've know."

"Different how?"

"I'll let you know when I figure it out," Lauren said, stepping to a curb packed with pedestrians, the proverbial sardine can of New Yorkers this busy area created.

"You know I'm not going to accept that answer."

The light remained red but people darted across the street anyway, dodging cars. "Yes, I know," Lauren assured her, as several people shoved her and Julie.

Julie grabbed Lauren to keep from falling. "Damn New Yorkers."

"We're New Yorkers," Lauren reminded her when a sharp burning sensation on her arm had her jerking to her left, to the many bodies surrounding her. "Ouch. Oh God." Her hand flew to the point of discomfort, pain radiating from hand to shoulder. "Damn, damn." She grabbed Julie's arm. "Don't cross. I need out of this crowd." She moved away from the curb, with Julie on her heels.

"What happened?" Julie asked urgently. "What's wrong?"

"I don't know." Lauren lifted her arm to show Julie, and pulled at her sleeve, trying to see the damage, and finding a large burn hole in the material.

"Holy moly," Julie said. "Some asshole burned you with a cigarette. I swear it looks like someone shoved it at you and held it there. Your sleeve is too poufy for it to get to your skin easily."

"Apparently it's not."

"We need to get you some ice quickly. Those kinds of burns hurt like a bitch. I know. My mom smokes and I landed at the end of her cigarette more than once as a kid."

Lauren looked down at her throbbing arm, the pain growing with each passing second. The hole in her sleeve seemed overly large, and she suddenly wasn't so sure this was an accident or a cigarette at all. "Ice." Lauren agreed. "Yes. I need ice."

"Damn cigarette smokers," Julie muttered. "Why in the hell does a person light up in a crowd like that?" She paused, her brows dipping. "You okay, sweetie? You're really pale."

Nodding, Lauren tried a smile but failed. "It's easing up," she lied. "It felt like I got stuck with a huge pin or something only the prick never stopped hurting."

Julie pulled back the silk of her shirt. "Dang Lauren, that burn is deep. I'm not sure it was a cigarette. Let's grab a cab and go to the ER."

"No," Lauren said, knowing she couldn't miss work before her trial. "I have some Advil in my purse, and I can get some ice at the restaurant. If it still hurts after that I'll consider it. It's feeling better already."

Julie didn't look convinced. "Are you sure?"

"I'm sure." Only she wasn't sure. She wasn't sure at all.

***

Dirt Diver was already sitting at a corner table of Lauren's favorite restaurant, out of her line of sight, when she and her friend walked in. Lauren was nothing, if not predictable.

He watched her slide into her booth, holding her arm where he'd taken his military issue mobile welder and scored her a new tattoo. Burned like hell, he bet. Well, that's what the little bitch deserved. Tear her down, one piece at a time. That was Dirt Diver's plan but it was proving so damn easy, even with her new boyfriend, that he was quickly becoming bored. He was going to fix that, though. He was going to give himself a challenge and prove to her just how vulnerable she was, how much it sucked to feel like a victim that couldn't escape her torture. Because he was that good. He could let her nestle down in the Walker Brothers' castle, let her pull down her guard, and feel safe, and still destroy her.

It was time to turn this into a full-fledged nightmare.

CHAPTER
TWELVE

Lauren sat in the corner booth of her favorite lunch spot, and instead of anticipating the first bite of the heavenly chocolate cake the place was famous for, she fantasized about the ice Julie was scavenging for her.

"Here you go," Julie said, sliding into the seat across from Lauren. "Relief is here."

Lauren held it to her arm. "Thank you."

"No problem. And I ordered our usual. I wasn't sure if you would be up to staying long, so I thought we should rush the food."

Lauren felt the chill on her arm, a slow numbness easing the pain. "This helps." Her attention locked on a familiar face. "Isn't that David Sullivan?"

Julie turned in her seat. "Where?"

"Too late. You can't see him anymore." Lauren made a face. "Weird though. I know that was him. He looked right at me and pretended not to see me."

Julie gave Lauren a hard stare. "Of course he did. You prosecuted the biggest case of his career, and he lost."

"And so he avoids me?"

"He was passed over as partner after losing the case. I'm pretty sure he thinks you ruined his life."

Lauren's eyes went wide. "I did not ruin his life. That's like blaming you for breaking up the marriages you legally dissolved."

The waitress appeared and set their food down in front of them, forcing Julie to put her reply on hold. The minute the woman walked away, Julie leaned forward, her voice low. "Of course you didn't ruin his life. But you know how people can be. They look for someone to blame and since I went out with one of his buddies a few years back, I happen to know he blames you. He's a big blame thrower, that guy." She stabbed a piece of chicken on top of her salad.

"Why didn't you tell me this?"

"I didn't tell you because I knew it would upset you, just like it clearly is now. I knew you'd tear yourself up over it."

This day was not going well. Her world felt like it was imploding on her. Her idea of getting out of the office and not letting fear control her certainly had backfired.

She shoved her plate aside, knowing she should have listened to Royce. "I'm going to the ladies' room." She dropped the bag of ice on the table, and grabbed a napkin to soak up the water on her arm. "Get my salad to go, will you?"

Fortunately, the restroom was empty, and she had a few blessed moments alone. She dried her shirt the best she could, her mind a jumbled mess. It was hard enough to put someone on death row, regardless of their crime. She really didn't need the added weight of other types of guilt. Like being told she'd ruined the life of her opposing counsel.

Several people funneled into the restroom, eyeing Lauren's

arm with interest. So much for her escape. She headed for the door, pushed it open, and ran straight into a hard wall of muscle, and when she might have flinched and pulled back, her nostrils flared with a familiar spicy scent of man.

"Royce," she breathed out, relaxing into him. "Oh, thank God, it's you."

He guided her into a corner, hands settling on her waist. Reaching up he brushed a piece of hair out of her eyes. "Julie said you were burned. Let me look at your arm."

Lauren felt her lips quiver as she nodded. "You had me followed, didn't you? That's how you're here?"

He glanced up at her. "Yes, and I'm pissed as hell that you left the building. However, I'll save my lecturing—and there will be lecturing—for when we're alone and you're not in pain. But damn it, this isn't a cigarette burn and this wasn't an accident. What if he'd have used a knife under the cover of the crowd? You might not be here right now."

He was right. She knew he was right. "I thought you were saving this until later?"

"I am. I'm not even close to saying everything I have to say."

She let out a breath and let her lashes lower. "I deserve this. I was foolish." She swallowed hard. "I didn't want this to be real." Her gaze lifted and then louder, "I *didn't want* this to be real. I think... I was in denial."

"You're okay," he said, his voice softening with understanding. "That's all that matters. Right now, we need to get you to an ER."

"No. It's fine. I'm fine."

"No, you're not, and we both know it. You're scared. You're hurt. We're going to the ER."

"I'll end up in the newspaper.'"

"Then we'll find a private doctor, but you have to have this looked at."

"I so don't need this right before the trial, Royce. I'm behind. I'm not myself. I almost feel like I need to step aside, but it's too late now, it would hurt the case."

"Maybe that was the idea."

***

Two hours later, Lauren and Royce were finally back at her apartment, and he was doing a walk through for safety. Lauren had called Julie and explained everything that was going on, and she had eagerly agreed to pick up Lauren's work for her. She just hoped she arrived in time to get some work done. The day was all but lost and the pain meds were going to knock her out when she finally caved and took them. As it was, the antibiotics were making her nauseous, which was probably because she hadn't eaten at all.

Royce appeared in the hallway, and she felt a surge of relief when he gave her the 'thumbs up' to enter. She rushed forward and straight to her bedroom so she could change. She wanted out of the burned shirt so she could separate herself from threats and fears to focus on work.

Royce followed her, leaning on the door frame as she dug in her drawer for her sweats. They'd had a fight when he'd driven her to the doctor's office, rather than home. They'd barely spoken while they were there, but as her anger had faded, she felt him there, by her side, strong and comforting, and... it felt like a relationship. It felt... right.

She abandoned her drawer and sat down on the bed. "I'm sorry. I was such a witch earlier. I just…"

"Don't move, Lauren," Royce ordered sharply. "Don't even breath." He reached for his gun.

"What?" Lauren whispered urgently. "What's happening?"

"I'm going to explain but do not, I repeat, do not react. Don't move until I tell you to. Understand?" He was already closing in on her, one slow step at a time.

"Yes. Okay. Tell me!"

"There's a snake on your bed."

***

Royce stopped in front of Lauren, but he didn't look at her. He kept his eye on the snake, knowing it could easily be as deadly as it was unexpected. "Get ready to run. When I say to run, you get out of the apartment in case there are more snakes."

"Yes… yes, okay."

"I'll count to three. One. Two. Three." He shoved her aside and fired at the snake, but as he suspected, it moved and he missed. He grabbed a handful of the comforter and threw it over the snake and then fired over and over. He reloaded and yanked the comforter back, ready to fire, but thankfully, he didn't have to. There was a pile of dead snake in the bed.

"Lauren," he called, turning to find her standing in the doorway. "I told you to get out of here." He grabbed her and started walking towards the door, getting her the hell out of here, all but dragging her to the hallway. "Are you trying to get yourself killed today?"

She held up her phone. "I was afraid you'd get bitten and

seconds could mean life or death. You might be Mr. FBI, Royce Walker, but you can die just like the rest of us."

He stared at her a moment, her words sinking in and eating away at his anger. For the second time now, she'd tried to protect him. It defied anything he'd ever experienced with a woman and he liked how that felt.

He kissed her fast and hard on the lips. "Damn, I'm crazy about you, woman. Stay here, and since you often reinterpret my words to your own definition, that means *don't move.*" He turned to go back inside, when a thought stopped him dead in his tracks.

He scrubbed his face and considered a moment, before dialing Luke. "Someone left Lauren a snake for a present. I need someone over here to make sure there aren't any more."

"Holy fuck," Luke grumbled. "Is it poisonous?"

"I didn't ask it before I killed it." He glanced at Lauren. "But if it was, this is attempted murder."

"No," she mouthed. "No."

"I'll get someone over there right now," Luke said.

"And get Julie to bring Lauren's work, and some clothes, to my place. Lauren is coming home with me." He hung up.

"Murder? You think someone just tried to kill me?"

"Or scare the hell out of you." And he was going to make the SOB pay for it, too.

"It worked. It worked really well."

"I know, baby," he said, reaching for her and wrapping her in his arms. "We're going to get this asshole. You have my word. You just have to let me protect you. No more running off to lunch like you did today."

"No more running off period. Seriously, Royce. I might be

hard-headed, but I'm not an idiot. I'm going to trust you completely from now on."

She trusted him, and his secret pact with her father was going to be the poison that killed their relationship.

CHAPTER
THIRTEEN

An hour later, Royce had Lauren back at his place, and she was soaking in his bathtub, naked and trusting and everything he wanted in a woman, but just hadn't known it. Until now. Until Lauren. And instead of being with her, showing her, telling her, he was a room away, pacing his living room while Luke lounged on his brown leather couch.

"This is absolute hell," Royce murmured. "I'm lying to her and she trusts me. I have to talk to her."

"Not now," Luke said. "Not when she's in danger. You don't want her pushing you away and making it impossible to protect her. Besides, you left out information about her father," Luke said, sitting up and resting his elbows on his knees. "You didn't lie. She'll be upset, but she'll get over it. It's not like you slept with her best friend."

"No. Ironically, you did." He sat down on the arm of one of two leather chairs framing the couch, keeping an eye on the bedroom door directly across from him.

"I'll pretend you didn't just say that," Luke said. "But since you brought up Julie, when I called her to have her bring over Lauren's work, she told me that the attorney who defended

Sheridan was at the restaurant today. She thought it was a strange coincidence. Apparently, the Sheridan loss spiraled into a career disaster he blames Lauren for. I'm going to see him tomorrow. I'll send one of our guys to talk to Sheridan. A man about to be executed tends to get chatty."

"What about Sheridan's family?"

"There's a brother, that's it. I plan to check him out. There is also a woman."

Royce's brow inched upward. "He killed his wife. What woman are we talking about?"

"Some chick that started writing to him while he was in prison."

"Ah," Royce said. "Never have understood the jailhouse groupies. What's your take on her?"

"I don't think it's much of a lead. She broke off contact with him some six months ago, and is even pregnant now with some other dude's kid."

"I'm not sure that means squat in the world we live in."

"I'm going to check her out. But the way I see it, if Sheridan is involved, then he would probably have taken out a contract on Lauren. It's cleaner."

"Who says this isn't a contract? Maybe whoever hired this guy wants Lauren played with before she's killed. Maybe that's why this attorney Sullivan was there today. He was watching when she got burned, eating up her fear."

"I like it as a theory," Luke agreed. "I'm sold on a professional for hire. This person, who I'm calling a man, but could be a woman, hasn't made mistakes. He's invisible, even with a camera on. He knows what he's doing." His cell phone rang and he answered it, his gaze going to Royce's. "Yeah.

Thanks." He snapped the phone shut. "The snake wasn't poisonous."

"So, this guy's playing with her."

"Yeah," Luke said. "But there's more. The place was a regular radio shack. He's been watching her, recording her."

"Sonofabitch," Royce cursed. "Don't tell her that. She's scared enough. I should have guessed that. I mean, he got in for the snake. He had full access."

"We finally have a potential motive, a way the senator might fit into this," Luke said. "Get images of Lauren undressing, or doing any number of things, and then uses them to get something from the senator."

Royce's jaw tensed. "Images of me with Lauren. I handed this guy ammunition, if that is even what this is about. He could be a sick bastard who's obsessed with her, and he's made getting to her look like child's play."

"Which leads me to a manpower issue. Blake's dealing with the Rhode Island airport contract, so until he returns, I'm limited to what I can do. I need to bring one of our guys in on this. Kyle, Rick, and Daniel are free. Jesse is also free. Tommy and Daniel are both booked. Kyle dealt with the snakes and he's a tech expert. He's already involved."

"Kyle," Royce agreed. "I've known him for years. We worked together at the agency. He'll keep his mouth shut."

"Give me Rick, too. He can chase some of the pieces I'm putting together on the senator."

"Do it," Royce said. "We don't have time to spare."

The door to the master bedroom, which sat just off the main living room, and directly in front of Royce, squeaked open. Lauren stepped into the room, and damn if his cock didn't twitch at the sight of her in his t-shirt and oversized sweats. The darn things were rolled up at the knees and hanging on her, and yet, he wasn't sure he'd ever seen her look sexier.

She walked to the opposite chair and settled her hands on top. "Hope I'm not interrupting anything."

"No," Luke said, smiling. "Nothing private in this family." The doorbell rang and Royce didn't miss the subtle tension that rolled through his brother, before Luke stood up. "It's probably Julie. I'll let her in on my way out."

Lauren rounded the chair and sat down. "She acts just as odd when his name comes up."

"You noticed that," Royce said.

She nodded. "Oh, yeah."

"Hello, hello," Julie called, appearing with a box in hand. "I left a suitcase by the door with clothes and other important girl stuff." She hurried forward and left the rather large box on the coffee table, then gave Lauren a once over "But then who needs clothes when you can wear Royce's?" She laughed. "You look like a kid wearing grown up clothes." She sat down on the couch and glanced at Royce. "You are a big ol' boy aren't you? Better to kill snakes, I suppose." She eyed Lauren. "Maybe you should have him pay a visit to that angry dude Alice said visited you today."

"What angry 'dude'?" Royce asked, his gaze colliding with Lauren's. "And why don't I know about him?"

"I haven't had time to tell you."

"Ah, hmmm," Julie said. "I was just trying to lighten the mood. I didn't mean to cause trouble."

"You have to make time, Lauren," Royce growled. "Someone could well be trying to kill you."

"Don't, Royce," Lauren said tightly. "Not now."

"Now," he insisted.

She inhaled and let it out. "He's the brother of the woman I'm prosecuting for the poisoning. He got pretty nasty. He—"

"Name," Royce said.

Her jaw tensed. "Jonathan Wilkins, and you're acting like a caveman."

"A caveman trying to keep you alive. This escalated to way beyond a few phone calls today, Lauren. Did he threaten you?"

"No. Not really. He was just very aggressive. Family members get that way, Royce. I'm used to it."

"Did you *feel* threatened?" he asked.

She hesitated. "I was on edge."

"Did you feel threatened?"

"Damn it, yes, but I told you. I was on edge. It wasn't long after we had our little," she stopped herself mid-sentence. "It was right after you dropped me at work."

He pushed to his feet. "Make time to tell me these things, Lauren. One mistake, one missed clue, could be critical. I'm going to talk to Luke. Don't open the door to anyone." He glanced at Julie. "Knock on Luke's door before you leave. I don't want you walking to your car alone." He headed for the door, not giving her a chance to answer.

"Wow," he heard Julie say softly, but not soft enough. "He's a big sexy, grizzly alpha of a man, isn't he? I know how the sexy is working out for you, but how's the grizzly alpha thing going?"

Royce didn't allow himself to hear the answer, he couldn't risk the distraction, or his reaction. He pushed open the door and locked it before pulling it shut, with one focus. Protecting Lauren, so that when this was over, she could scream and shout and kick him to the curb if she so wished. All that mattered was keeping her safe and alive.

***

After spending a good hour that she should have been working talking with Julie, Lauren dove into her work, ignoring the rumble of her stomach and the throb of her arm. The Advil Julie had brought her had worked for all of half an hour, so she popped some aspirin she found in Royce's bathroom cabinet. She had to try and get some work done before she took the more powerful pain medication the doctor had given her.

She picked up the box of her work from the coffee table and walked to the large oak desk that set just off the living area, and by the kitchen door. She set it down at her feet and started pulling out her files, remarkably comfortable in her sexy grizzly alpha's home. She smiled at Julie's creative description, thankful for a good friend who could make a smile possible at a time like this. Lauren wasn't sure who was more surprised, her or Julie, over just how much Lauren liked her alpha male's alpha side.

A loud sound filled the silence of the room and Lauren jumped to her feet, her heart thundering in her ears, to scan the room. The sound clamored again and her gaze riveted to the fireplace opposite the couch, air rushing from her lungs. It was the clock above the mantel chiming. Oh yeah, she was rattled all right. She sank back to the leather chair beneath her and wished Royce would return. Being alone wasn't all that appealing right now. She unloaded her files onto the desk, deciding work would be the best distraction, but pausing at the smaller letter-sized flat box Alice had told her about.

She sighed and snatched a letter opener to break the seal down the middle. Though she knew what the reports were supposed to say, she never took a verbal as final when headed into trial. She flipped open the double-sided lid and stared at the contents, her heart dropping to her stomach. A calendar page lay on top with today's date marked off.

"Don't touch it," she whispered to herself and stood up, afraid something was going to explode or bite her or... she took off running for the door. Once she was there, she fumbled with the lock. "Damn, damn open!" It jerked towards her and she burst into the hallway, her bare feet padding on the wooden floor, as she started yelling, "Royce! Royce!"

The door down the hallway opened and Luke appeared, rushing toward her, grabbing hold of her, and pulling a gun from somewhere. "Talk to me, Lauren. What's happening?"

"Lauren!" Royce shouted charging up the stairwell.

Lauren tore herself away from Luke and threw herself at Royce. He folded her into his big, powerful arms. "Package," she managed to get out. "There's a package. It was delivered to my office and Julie brought it and I opened it..."

"What's inside?" he demanded quickly.

"A calendar page and I don't know what else. I didn't touch it. What does this person want from me? Why won't they just leave me alone?"

"Where is it?" Luke asked from behind her.

Lauren turned in time to see Luke holster his gun at his ankle, under his pants. "The desk. It's open on the desk."

He lifted his chin at Royce. "I'll check it out."

"Be careful," Lauren said. "Please be careful, Luke."

"Careful is my middle name."

"He'll be okay," Royce said, pulling her against him. "And so will you."

Lauren melted into Royce, and for the first time in her life, she felt more secure in a man's arms than she did on her own.

CHAPTER
FOURTEEN

Thirty minutes after the discovery of the box, Lauren stood in Royce's kitchen, staring at the twenty newspaper clippings from her various trials, all spread out on the table.

"Is there anything in all of this that rings a bell?" Royce asked. "There's a message here. We need to try to understand what it is."

Lauren sank down into a chair and pressed her hands to the side of her face. "Other than he's been watching me for a long time and wants me to know, no. Nothing else comes to mind. They're random trials over the course of years."

"Are they all after the Sheridan trial?" Luke asked.

"Sheridan was one of my first cases," she said. "So yes. These are all after Sheridan. As you can see, I've put plenty of people behind bars that probably hate me. Heck, if I get through this, there could easily be another."

"Which is why we aren't going to the police," Royce said. "They won't be much help and we don't want to give anyone else the idea of lashing out at you."

"Maybe this was to confuse us," Luke said. "To give us a lot of suspects."

"I've never questioned why I do what I do," Lauren said. "Not until now. Now... I don't know what I'm supposed to do. How do I live like this?" She laughed without humor. "This is the payment I get for putting criminals behind bars? Stalked and threatened and twisted in knots? What if I had kids or siblings or a husband? I'd be terrified they'd be in danger. Maybe my father is right. Maybe this is fool's work."

Royce squatted down beside her. "You're one of the brave and caring people who try to make a difference in this world. There is nothing foolish about that."

Luke cleared his throat. "I'll leave you two alone."

Lauren looked at him. "Thank you for everything you are doing, Luke. I mean that. You don't have to help me, but you are."

He gave her a bow. "My pleasure. And for the record, I'm with Royce. You're brave. Stay that way. Don't give into the monsters or they'll take over."

"Oh, God. Julie. What if he targets Julie?"

"I already thought of that," Luke said. "I have her being watched."

Lauren sighed. "Oh, thank you, Luke."

He gave her a salute and headed out of the kitchen.

"I'm going to make you something to eat," Royce said. "Then you're going to take a pain pill and sleep."

"I'm too tired to be hungry."

"You need to eat a little something." He kissed the tip of her nose. The phone on the wall rang and he smiled. "Some of us still use our house phones."

"I plan to rip mine out of the wall." The phone kept ringing. "Are you going to answer it?"

"I have a machine." He pushed to his feet. "And feeding you is more important. I have sandwiches and not much else though, I'm afraid." The machine beeped. "Royce, call your mother. Why don't you ever answer your phone?" He backed up and grabbed the receiver, before saying, "I told you I never answer this phone. You have to call my cell."

Lauren smiled weakly, feeling a punch in her gut, a bit of envy. What she wouldn't do to have her mother alive right now. She turned back to the table, pulling one of the clippings forward, and started reading before moving to the next.

Before she knew what was happening, Royce was sitting down next to her and there were plates on the table. "I didn't even know when you got off the phone."

"Or when I asked you if ham and Swiss was okay," he commented.

"I just kept reading and thinking I'd find something in one of the clippings that would set off a light bulb." She took a bite of the sandwich and then reached for the soda Royce had apparently set in front of her as well.

"And while you're thinking about that, you aren't thinking about your current case."

"So you think it's about my current case?"

"In my experience, the obvious usually is the right choice. The rest is a distraction."

"So what do I do?"

"You go to sleep tonight and you wake up fresh and you win this case. I'll take you to work and I'll have people watching you while Luke and I dig into ending this once and for all. Luke was right, Lauren. You can't let this monster, or any for that matter, win. You do your thing, sweetheart, and I'll do mine. We'll get our man and you'll get your conviction."

Lauren felt her eyes prickle and tears well by her lashes.

"Wow," Royce said, pulling her into his lap and thumbing away her tears. "What just happened?"

"I don't know. I'm tired. I'm not even a crier. You and your family are so close, and so good to me." She pressed her hand to his cheek. "No one but my mother and Julie has ever told me to fight for what I believe in and they'd fight with me. Never."

"And never has a woman made me want to be there for her like you do, Lauren." Royce kissed her, tasted her tears and her fears, and her passion, and admitted what he'd known from that first night with her. He was falling in love.

He picked her up and she wrapped her legs around his waist, burying her face in his neck as he carried her to his bedroom. His bedroom. He laid her down on the bed and stripped her naked, kissing her, touching her, taking his time to properly make love to her. And when he finally entered her, when their eyes locked, he knew that not only was he going to fight by her side, he was going to fight to make her his woman.

FIFTEEN

The next morning, Royce pulled to the curb in front of Lauren's building, making sure she was safely at work before he set off into action. Sitting outside Lauren's building while she worked wasn't going to end this for her.

"Remember, I have two men already in position here at the building. You have both of their numbers on auto-dial. Be aware of what's going on but don't let it consume you. You're safe." He glanced down at the deep cleavage of the emerald blouse she wore under a black suit. "From everyone but me."

She tugged at the blouse. "Leave it to Julie to bring me the most inappropriate clothes she owns. I'll be pinning this shut."

"We can go get your clothes tonight on the way home."

"Home?" she asked.

"I've got you with me," he said, pulling her close and kissing her. "Don't expect me to let you go."

She wiped his mouth. "Pink isn't your color."

He smiled and kissed her again. "Text me when you get to your office so I know you're safe."

She nodded and reached for the door. "Be careful."

"Careful is my middle name."

She smiled. "Funny. I thought it was Luke's." She pushed open the door and slung her briefcase over her shoulder, before heading the short distance to the glass door and disappearing inside.

He dialed Kyle. "I'm leaving."

"I'm about to follow her onto the elevator. She'll be fine." He hung up, no doubt already inside the car with Lauren.

Royce dropped his phone on the seat, his gut tight. Damn, this was killing him. He was going to enjoy tracking down this bastard. His first target: the 'dude' who'd been nasty to Lauren the day before. Whether he was guilty of being a jerk or guilty of more, he'd know not to bother Lauren again when Royce was done with him.

Fifteen minutes later, Royce pulled into an apartment in the east side, poverty-stricken section of Brooklyn and made his way to the door 4B. He knocked, and mumbled under his breath, "Come on, you son of a bitch. Answer."

The door swung revealing a man wearing jeans and nothing more. "Yeah?"

A standoff ensued. They stared at each other, sizing each other up. Cockiness, bred from Special Forces training, oozed from his opponent. The man was a deadly weapon, but then, so was he. "Jonathan Wilkins?"

"You're looking at him," Wilkins said. "Who are you and what do you want?"

"The name's Royce Walker. I'd like to talk about Lauren Reynolds."

No reaction. "What about her?"

"You tell me."

"I hate the bitch. What's it to you?"

"Everything."

"She's trying to kill my sister," he said coldly.

"She's doing her job."

"Amazing how some people get paid to kill another while others just get thrown in jail, now isn't it?" There was no mistaking the malice to the question. "Makes a person appreciate the laws of another country. An eye for an eye. A life for a life."

"That's called the death penalty," Royce reminded him.

"And here we get a jury and we're innocent until proven guilty."

"She's already convicted my sister, and we both know it."

"Her opinion doesn't matter. The jury's does."

"And she tells them what she wants them to hear."

He started to shut the door and Royce shoved his foot in the door. "Touch her and you'll regret it."

"I'm shaking in my bare feet, man. Absolutely quivering. I'm put in my place."

They glared at one another and Royce wanted to yank the asshole into the hallway and beat him to a pulp, but he wouldn't do Lauren any good in jail. However, if this guy meant her harm, he needed him to know that she wasn't alone, that she was protected. "I'm going to be watching you," he said, and stepped back.

Wilkins's lips lifted in an evil smile. "Enjoy the show." And he shut the door.

***

Royce was halfway back to the city, heading to Sullivan's offices, the attorney who'd defended Sheridan, when it hit him that he'd never told Wilkins who he was, beyond a name, and Wilkins had never asked. Something about that rubbed him wrong, but then, everything about Wilkins rubbed him wrong.

He sent a text to Lauren and made sure she was okay, then called Julie. "Law offices."

"I need to speak to Julie Morrison."

"She's not available," the prim voice on the other line informed him.

He held his tone in check with effort, but his words still held a sharp edge. "Make her available. Tell her Royce Walker needs to speak to her urgently."

"Sir—"

"Just do it," he demanded. Rude and he knew it, but damn it, he didn't have niceties in him right now. Instantly he heard office music in his ear.

"Royce?" Julie said, concern in her voice. "Is Lauren okay?"

"Yes," he said reassuring her, feeling a bit of guilt for scaring her. "I just need you to take her lunch and check on her."

A sigh of relief escaped Julie's lips. "That's an order I'll happily take. You really are a bossy bear, Royce."

"Yeah, I know. I'm trying to work on that. Have her call me when you get there. I mean, please have her call me when you get there."

She laughed. "Since you asked, I absolutely will." She paused. "Don't hurt her, Royce. She deserves to be happy."

His gut knotted. "I know. Believe me, I know."

By the time Royce parked his truck and fed a parking meter, he knew he would be hard pressed to make his meeting with Luke after this trip. Sullivan's street level office was small and rather humble in decor, at least from the exterior. A doorbell chimed as he entered. The lobby hosted a light assortment of furnishings including a well-worn desk and several mix and match pictures. It was a far cry from the elite law firm Sullivan had worked for during the Sheridan trial.

A tall man with curly blond hair, a lanky build, and a suspicious gaze appeared in a corner doorway. With sleeves a hint too long, and pants the same, his suit fit him about as well as the furnishings. It didn't. There was an air about this man that said money. A complete contradiction to his surroundings.

"Can I help you?"

"I'm looking for Sullivan. David Sullivan."

"I'm Sullivan. Who are you?"

Royce sensed nervousness in the man. "Royce Walker. I handle security issues for individuals as well as businesses. I'm here to discuss Marvin Sheridan." It wasn't a request, nor was it meant to be.

"What of him?" he questioned with narrowed eyes.

"There is suspicion that he could be involved in some threats one of my clients has been receiving."

Sullivan studied Royce for several long moments as if he was deciding if he should talk to him. Finally, with a nod, he said, "Come this way," turned and started walking.

Odd man, he thought, following him, noting the man's jerky movements, almost like a machine fighting a mechanism.

Inside the corner office, Sullivan sat behind a bigger version of the scuffed piece of wood in the center of the lobby. Royce settled into a worn blue cloth visitor's chair. He would have preferred to stand but he sensed Sullivan's unease and didn't want to intimidate him by hovering. He wanted the man to talk.

Leaning back, Sullivan rocked in a squeaky leather chair. Like nails on a chalkboard, the sound raked on Royce's nerves.

"Sheridan is scheduled to be executed," he said. "What harm is he to your client?"

Royce narrowed his gaze on the man. "Kept up with him, I see?"

"Wouldn't you if you were the attorney who defended a man being put to death?"

Royce shrugged. "He's a killer."

"He was temporarily insane."

"The jury said differently."

Tapping the fingers of one hand on his desk, Sullivan studied Royce. "What are you after here, Mr. Walker?"

"How do you feel about Lauren Reynolds?"

"Is Lauren your client?"

"My client's identity is confidential. Again, how do you feel about Lauren Reynolds?"

"How does anyone feel about the opponent that brings them to their knees?" His tone was hostile.

"You tell me," Royce challenged.

"It doesn't really matter. It's past history."

"What does that mean?"

Sullivan snorted. "What do you think it means? The man is going to die, end of story. He's out of appeals."

"How's Sheridan handling that?"

Sullivan raked a hand through his hair. "He's accepting. He met a woman who helped him find God. He says he's been forgiven and ready to face his maker."

"Should you have won the case?"

A frown dipped his brows. "Should have, yes."

"Why didn't you?" Royce pressed.

His fist balled on top of the desk. "I had some bumps during the trial, and Lauren Reynolds milked each and every one of them. Surely you read the press I got over the ordeal. I lost my job, my wife, everything."

"And you blame her?"

He grimaced and seemed to stiffen. "I did, but not anymore. I stumbled. She did what any good attorney would do and took advantage of opportunity. There's no room in the courtroom to screw up. You just can't do it."

Royce stood to leave. "One more thing," he said. "Is there anyone around Sheridan who might want revenge on his behalf?"

"Other than me and the ten partners in the law firm I worked for, no one."

Ten partners who had suffered the bad press of losing the trail. Damn, the list of possibilities just got longer and longer. Royce turned to leave. "There is one more person who hates Lauren," Sullivan said. Royce turned and arched a brow.

"My ex-wife. She lost all the prestige and money she thought I was about to give her. The bitch married me for money and power, and nothing more."

CHAPTER
SIXTEEN

In a few short hours, Lauren had negotiated plea bargains on four cases. She was zapped and she still had hours of work to do. It was taking every ounce of concentration she had to keep focused on the words she was reading as she clicked through her e-mail. She had forty new items in her inbox since she'd cleared it two hours before.

"Lauren."

Lauren jumped at the unexpected, familiar voice of her ex-fiancé, Roger. "You scared the heck out of me. How did you get past the front desk?"

He leaned against the door frame, looking every bit like Tom Cruise in 'The Firm', one leg crossed over the other, his thousand dollar suit fitted, his hair and nails perfectly groomed. "She was on the phone and I waved and walked by."

So easily. Too easily. She was fooling herself to think she was safely nestled in her office. "What are you doing here, Roger?"

"What kind of way is that to greet your ex-fiancé? I am, after all, the man you almost pledged never-ending love to."

"I'm tired. I have a big trial starting, and I don't have time for this." She refocused on her computer screen, intent on dismissing him.

"I worry about you."

The sincerity in his voice surprised her. She gave him a curious look. Suddenly, the past came back in a rush of memories, but none of them were good. She couldn't remember why she'd ever said 'yes' to marrying him.

"We weren't meant to be, Roger. We were a business arrangement and neither of us would have been happy long term."

Lauren's buzzer went off. She punched the button. "Yes."

"Pick up."

Lauren frowned, but reached for the receiver. "Yes?"

Alice whispered urgently, "There is a very large, very grouchy man here who insists on seeing you."

Lauren couldn't help but laugh. "That's Royce. Tell him I'll be right out." Lauren pushed to her feet. "I have a visitor I need to attend to."

Abruptly Roger closed the distance between them, and was behind her desk, his hands on her shoulders, right over the bandage and her burn. "I made a mistake. I had cold feet. We can make it work. I'll make it up to you."

Lauren grabbed his hand. "You're hurting me."

"And you're destroying me. I miss you. I—"

"Let her go."

Roger released her and turned to the door, where Royce stood, tall and broad, in jeans and a T-shirt that might as well have been leather and knives, for the look on his face.

"Who are you?" Roger demanded.

"The only man who gets to touch her."

Lauren gaped at the caveman-like statement. "Royce," she

ground out between her teeth.

"Yes, sweetheart?"

"I was just leaving," Roger said, but Royce still blocked the doorway and made no effort to move.

"Don't leave on my account," Royce said in a hard voice Lauren was starting to worry about.

Roger, who was used to being under fire in the courtroom appeared to recover from his initial shock. Offering a cool glare, he said, "I'm not. I simply came by to check on Lauren." He glanced at Lauren, "I'll call you," and then stepped forward as if daring Royce to block his way.

For several tense seconds, Lauren thought Royce wasn't going to move, but finally he backed up to let Roger pass. She was at the door when Royce stepped inside her office, shutting the door. "You're the only man who gets to touch me? I'm not your property, Royce."

"No. But we're either exclusive or we aren't anything."

At any other time, she'd have reveled in what he was saying, what he was offering, but not now, not like this. "You don't get to tell me we're exclusive. You don't get to demand it. That's not how this works."

He grabbed her and picked her up, setting her on the desk, shoving her skirt up and pressing her legs apart to stand between them. His hands framed her body, pressed to the wooden surface beside her hips. "Do you want Roger?"

Heat sizzled down her spine. This damnable alpha side of him pissed her off, but it turned her on too, and she didn't understand why. She pressed on his hard, unmoving chest. "Don't bully me or push me around. Let me up."

"Do you want Roger?"

"You know I don't."

"Apparently you want to keep you options open," he said, his hands skimming up her thighs. "You don't want to say we're exclusive. So maybe this is just a good time ride for you?"

"You're being an asshole," she said. "Demanding and demanding. You don't get to demand. You ask, Royce."

His eyes darkened, glinting dangerously. "You want me to ask?" He skimmed his thumb over her panties. "How about this? Will you come for me, Lauren? Right here, in your office?" He slid his fingers under her panties and she gasped at the pleasure. "Does he make you wet like this?"

"Stop it, Royce," she gasped as his fingers pushed inside her. "Stop."

He reached up and tugged down her blouse, exposing her bra and then her nipple, before leaning down and licking it. "Not until you say you're mine."

"I'm not saying that. I won't ever be yours if you're this big of an asshole."

"I'm just making sure you know who is supposed to be fucking you."

She arched against his fingers, unable to stop herself. "I hate how you're acting." She buried her face in his shoulder. "I hate that you're doing... this." Her body clenched around his fingers, pleasure rushing through her, defying her words.

The fingers of his other hand tangled into her hair, forcing her gaze to his, her mouth a breath from his. He stroked her clit with his thumb, pumping inside her. "I hate the idea of him doing this to you."

"He can't do this to me."

"Why?" he all but growled.

There was something in his voice, in his words, a vulnerability that defied his demands that reached into her and drew a response. "Because he's not you, Royce."

He kissed her, hard and demanding, a fierce claiming that had her moaning and giving into her need for him. Everything blurred then turned into shades of pleasure. She couldn't get enough of him, she couldn't even remember where she was. Only that she helped him shove his pants down, welcomed him ripping away her panties, and whimpered when his cock pressed into her.

He thrust into her, lifted her off the desk, and pulled her down on him. She clung to him, hungered for him like she had never another man, and yes, she came for him, just like he wanted her to.

He shook with his release and then set her on the desk, burying his face in her neck. Emotions rolled over Lauren and she didn't know what she was feeling. "Let me up," she said, shoving on his shoulders. "I need up. Someone could walk in."

He lifted his head and looked like he would refuse, a moment before he pulled a tissue from the box on her desk, handed it to her, and pulled out of her.

Lauren quickly gave him her back to clean up. She snatched her panties, shoved them in her desk drawer and fixed her shirt. She turned to find him standing close, hands pressed in his pockets.

"I'm sorry," he said softly. "I don't know what the hell came over me. I don't want anyone else to touch you and I'm pretty sure I just screwed this up in every possible way."

The raw vulnerability in him she'd sensed minutes before reached out to her, "I don't want Roger. I don't want anyone else, but if you act like that again," she hesitated, "I might come, but I won't like it."

His lips turned up slowly. "You won't like it?"

"Okay, I might like it, but I won't be happy I liked it."

He bit back a broader smile. "Do I dare believe that comment means you forgive me?"

"Yes, but—"

He was holding her before she could add, "Don't go caveman on me again."

"Never?" he teased.

She brushed her fingers over his. "Maybe later tonight, but not after that."

He chuckled. "I can't wait."

And neither could she. It was time to face the very real possibility that she'd gone and exposed herself to more than a dangerous monster trying to kill her. She'd exposed her heart. Lauren was falling in love with Royce.

CHAPTER
SEVENTEEN

I t was near midnight and Royce lay in his bed, Lauren snuggled to his side sleeping, something he couldn't seem to manage. Three days had passed, and despite his caveman behavior at her office, as Lauren often called it, or perhaps because of it, she'd changed, let down her guard with him. She finally seemed to get how much he was invested in what was going on with them. Any happiness he might have arrived at was diminished by the torment of knowing that he was failing to protect her, proven by the fact that every day came with another calendar sheet delivered by what seemingly was a damn ghost. One had been stuffed in a lunch bag from a delivery to her office, but no one at the restaurant claimed to have put it there. One had been on his truck window despite the video footage that showed nothing. The final one had been left with the security desk at her building, delivered by a little old lady who disappeared, and was never seen again. And every single delivery was a taunt that said, "I can get to her whenever I want to", and Royce knew it.

His cell phone started to vibrate on the bedside table and he grabbed it, certain a call at this hour wasn't good. Lauren's head popped up. "What time is it?"

"Late," he said, answering the call that the ID identified as Bill Smith, the Senator's staff security person.

"What's wrong?" he asked, not bothering with 'hello.' He untwined himself from Lauren to sit up, anticipating trouble and heading to his closet.

"Senator Reynolds' house is on fire."

Royce stopped in his tracks. "How?"

"I'm not there yet but I'm being told it's obvious arson."

Holy hell. "Is everyone okay?"

"The senator certainly is, enough so that he's yelling at me and telling me I need to get my ass over here and start doing my job. He wants you there. That's an order."

An order. Right. He didn't even work for the man. "I'll be there in a few minutes." He ended the call and dialed Luke, managing to get his pants on while it rang. "Get over here, dressed, and ready to leave. And get Blake down here to stay with Lauren." He didn't wait for a reply, ending the call and reaching for a shirt and pulling it over his head.

"What's happening?" Lauren asked, on her knees now and clutching the blanket. "What's wrong? Is everyone okay?"

Damn, he didn't want to tell her this. He grabbed his boots and headed for the bed. "No one is hurt." He sat down next to her. "Everyone is completely fine." He quickly put on his boots and ran his hands down his pants.

"But? I hear the 'but'. What is going on?"

"I'm going to repeat this to make sure I'm making myself clear. Everyone is okay, but there has been a fire at your father's house."

"What? How? Oh, God. I have to get over there." She

shoved away the blanket and he shackled her arm.

"No," he said. "You need to stay here. I need to know you're safe so I can deal with your father."

"Why do you need to deal with my father? He's *my* father." She frowned. "Why did he call you?"

"That was Bill, his security guy."

"I don't understand. Why did Bill call *you*?"

He wasn't going to lie to her. He hadn't done so before now, and doing so would only make her think worse of him later. "It's complicated. Too complicated to explain at this moment. I know you're worried, but everyone is safe. It's you who might not be if you're there, in the middle of all the chaos, where you're an easy target."

"I don't understand what's going on." She shook her head. "I... what aren't you telling me?"

"I promise you that I will explain everything when I get back." He caressed her cheek. "Please, baby. I'm begging you here. No caveman routine. No demands. *I'm asking.* Let me deal with this without worrying about you."

"I don't want to stay here."

"I know. And I wouldn't ask you to, not under these circumstances, if I didn't really feel like it was important."

She considered him a long moment. "Fine. Yes. But only if you call me when you get there. I want to know you've seen my father with your own two eyes and that he's really okay."

"I will." He leaned in and kissed her, and his gut clenched. He hesitated, knowing this was the wrong time to tell her how he felt, but afraid not to. She was going to find out about his deal with her father tonight, he just knew it, and she was going to hate him.

Knocking sounded from the front door and he silently cursed. "I have to go." He kissed her again and took off for the other room, forcing himself to leave her.

**

Lauren walked to the living room, shoving her arms in her red silk robe, only to come face to face with Blake. He stood by the couch, fully dressed, his long hair wild and loose around his shoulders, his eyes blurry with barely escaped sleep.

They stared at each other several beats, before he said, "Not the best circumstances to get to know each other, but I've always found the best way to get past niceties and awkward shit is food." He motioned to the kitchen. "Want to go raid the fridge with me?"

She sighed, surprised and relieved at how easily he'd torn away the tension. "There's leftover pizza, but I get the cheese slices."

He grinned, his brown eyes friendly, warm. "Deal."

A few minutes later they sat at the coffee table, eating cold pizza and drinking soda, both of them with their cell phones lying on the table. "How's your arm?" he asked.

"Much better. It's going to scar but I can live with that." She dropped a piece of crust into the box. "Do you think the same person set the fire?"

"Yes." He sucked down some drink.

"You don't candy coat things, I see."

"Nope." He reached for another slice of pizza.

"Aren't you ATF or ex-ATF? Shouldn't you be at the fire?"

"I don't know the people involved the way Royce and Luke

do."

"You mean my father."

"And the suspects."

"What suspects." Her stomach fell to her feet. "You mean you think this involves me, don't you?"

He moved the empty pizza box. "Don't you?"

She swallowed hard. "I... I didn't know we thought the fire was intentional."

"It was."

The phone in the kitchen rang and Lauren started to get up. "It's not him," Blake said. "He never answers that phone or calls it. I don't know why he has the damn thing." He reached under the coffee table and pulled out a deck of cards. "You're not going to sleep. We might as well play."

"I wish he'd call."

"He'll call," Blake said. "But once you get on a scene things tend to get crazy."

"What if he's wrong and my father is hurt?"

He grabbed his phone. "I'll call Luke if it will make you feel better."

"Thank you, Blake."

Luke answered almost immediately and Blake quickly told Lauren, "Your father is fine. He's currently yelling at Royce, which is why he hasn't called us." He chatted with Luke a moment and then hung up. "Before you ask, I have no idea why your father is yelling at Royce. But yelling means he's alive and kicking and isn't that all that really matters?"

"What if his house had been burned down because of me? What if someone would have died?"

"Those things didn't happen." He studied her a long

moment. "Take it from me, Lauren. 'What if' will eat you alive. Don't do that to yourself."

He was talking about what happened to his fiancée; she knew he was.

He grabbed the cards. "Since we don't have 'Old Maid,' how about 'Go Fish'?"

"Go Fish," she said. "That's a walk down childhood lane. I'm in." She'd do anything to keep from climbing the walls. "Let me go put on some coffee first."

Lauren headed to the kitchen and quickly started to load the coffee pot, realizing just how comfortable she was here, how at home she felt in Royce's place. He felt right. They felt right. She flipped the pot on and promised herself she wasn't going to read into what was happening tonight, or his promise to tell her everything, that inferred he'd been keeping something from her.

The phone on the wall rang again about the time that she reached for two coffee mugs in the cabinet, and it hit her that it was the middle of the night. Who called at a time like this? Her nerves prickled, worry filling her. When she would have headed back to the living room, she just stood there, waiting on the machine, certain the ticking clock had found her. The beep sounded and a voice came on the line instead.

"Royce, sugar," a female purred. "Donna here. Where have you been, baby? Call me so we can do dinner or whatever else you want to do." Lauren clenched the cups, feeling her chest tighten with emotion, a flashback of finding Roger in bed with another woman turning into an image of Royce with another woman.

"She's no one, Lauren," Blake said from behind her.

She whirled around to face him. "That didn't sound like no

one."

"She didn't even rate his cell phone number."

"So that's why he has a land line? For women."

"He was single and he had no interest in long term. You changed that, Lauren. You know you did. You're upset tonight. Don't make this something it's not."

She didn't know what she felt or what she thought. She only knew that everything was spinning out of control, that she had no control. She'd done what she'd never done in her life. She'd given it all away.

She pushed off the counter and walked toward him. "I'm going to my father's house." He blocked the exit. "Move, Blake. I'm sick of you Walker brothers pushing me around."

"He is crazy about you."

She wasn't going to cry. *She was not going to cry.* Her chin lifted. "You can take me where I want to go or I can call a cab. Your choice."

He scrubbed his hair. "Oh, well hell. He's going to take my head for this, but I'll take you."

***

The first thing Lauren saw when they rounded the neighborhood corner were fire trucks, the next was her father's house still looking normal and in one piece. She let out a breath of relief, especially since Blake had been desperately trying to warn Royce and Luke that they were on their way, and he couldn't seem to reach either of them.

"It's not on fire," Lauren said, glancing at Blake.

"It's contained," Blake said. "That doesn't mean it's not on fire, or it wasn't on fire." He dropped his phone to the seat, and grumbled something about hanging Royce up by his toes. "Looks like several houses down is as close as we're going to get with all the yellow tape." He angled the Ranger to back in between two cars, and put the car in reverse, pausing to say, "I'll go get Royce and bring him to—"

Lauren shoved open the door, hopped out, and started running toward the house, the cool night air whipping through her hair and making her pull the jacket of her sweat suit closer to her body.

"Lauren!" Blake shouted.

She ignored him, cutting up a line of bushes to avoid the cluster of four official personnel not far away, and then ducking under the tape.

Blake shouted again, getting closer, and Lauren stepped up her pace, and charged toward the porch. She hit the first step, relieved that if there was any structural damage, it wasn't significant enough to be seen from here.

She entered the front door, hearing Blake talking to someone behind her. She paused inside the foyer, seeing no obvious fire or damage, but the scent of smoke tainted the air, bitter proof there had been a fire. The sound of voices drew her to the left, toward her father's den.

Her tennis shoes padded soundlessly over the carpet and she paused at the cracked door, some invisible force, instinct, telling her to wait, to listen. She eased around the edge of the door so that she could see into the room.

Royce was standing by the marble fireplace, Luke at the opposite side. Her father, and some man she didn't recognize, sat in leather chairs framing the couch.

"I'm not going to keep this from her," Royce said. "I'm done, Senator. This ends tonight."

"You'll do no such thing," her father said, standing up. "When I hired you—"

"I don't work for you," he said. "I did you a favor because you saved my father's life in Vietnam. The end."

The words cut through Lauren and she acted immediately, shoving open the door and stepping inside, seeing only Royce. "Favor? I was a favor?"

"Lauren," Royce said, taking a step toward her. "I can explain."

"That's a 'yes,'" she said, humiliation and hurt pouring through her. She turned and started to run, bursting through the front door, rushing down the steps, and straight into the path of Blake. At the same moment, Royce's hand was on her arm, shooting hot fire through her body.

She whirled around to face him, jerking out of his grasp. "Don't touch me. You don't ever touch me again."

"Let me explain. Please. Just hear me out."

"You made a deal with my father," she said. "You used sex and my feelings to get inside my life to do his bidding whatever the hell it was. There's nothing you can say that I want to hear."

"He asked me to check out a couple threats against your life and I agreed. And I would have told you but I saw you were in danger and I wasn't going to risk you pushing me away."

"So you thought you'd just fuck me into submission?"

"No," he breathed out. "Damn it, no. This has been eating me alive. You had me at 'hello,' Lauren. Hell, you had me from across the room. I couldn't, I can't, let you push me away and end up dead. I won't let that happen."

"I'm not your concern. Not anymore."

"This wasn't a fire. It was a bomb, delivered in a package that said it was for you. It went off, sitting on a table in the dining room; thankfully when no one was around."

She gasped. "Oh God. I... I can't believe this is happening." Luke stepped to Royce's side. "Julie. I need to make sure Julie—"

"I know," Luke said. "Kyle tried to get her to my place. He's taking her to a well-secured hotel. Her choice."

She nodded. "Okay. Yes."

"And you're coming home with me," Royce said.

"No. I'm going to stay with Julie."

"Staying with Julie makes her more of a target," he said. "You have to see that."

"The police have to know about this now," she said. "I'll talk to them. I'm sure they want to talk to me. I'll get protection."

He closed the distance between them and pulled her into his arms, his face buried in her neck, lips by her ear. "I swear to you, Lauren, that if you don't leave here with me of your own free will, I will throw you over my shoulder and carry you out of here. Hate me if you have to but you're going to be alive when this is over."

She was trembling with his touch, with the warmth of his breath on her neck, with desire to turn back time and have him be who she'd thought he was. To have them be what she'd thought they were. "I can't. I just... can't."

"She can stay at my place tonight," Blake said from behind her. "Then you two can figure things out from there."

Royce pulled back to look at her, his blue eyes hard with determination. "Choose. Me or Blake?"

"Blake."

His chest expanded and then relaxed, before he took a step backwards. "We have to talk."

"No. No, we don't." She turned to Blake. "Please get me out of here."

His gaze lifted over her head to Royce's and held a long moment before he stepped aside and waved her forward.

Once they were in the Ranger, darkness and silence was all there was, until finally, they pulled into the garage of their building and parked.

They sat there a moment, neither of them moving. "When I was in the ATF I fell in love with a woman, another agent."

Shocked at his personal confession, she turned to look at him, but he wasn't looking at her. He was clutching the steering wheel, staring at the concrete wall in front of them.

"Yes," she said softly. "I... knew that."

"So you know she was murdered."

Her heart clenched. "Yes."

His head jerked around, his gaze piercing hers, even in the darkness of the vehicle. "If Royce had asked me if he should have come clean with you, I wouldn't have told him 'no' but 'hell no'. You would have done what you did tonight. You would have pushed him away and made it damn near impossible for him to protect you. And you don't take risks with someone's life, especially not someone you care about the way he cares about you. You risk their anger, their inability to forgive you, but *you don't* let them die."

She could barely breathe with his words. "You blame yourself. You think you compromised on something that cost her life."

"I know I did," he said. "I let her die. He's been a wreck,

worried you would hate him, worried about protecting you. And that woman on the machine was nothing to him, Lauren. Nothing. You are. He has a past, but so do you. We're going upstairs and you aren't staying with me. You're staying with him. If you want to sleep in the guest room, then so be it, but you need to be with him, so you two can try and work this out."

She started to cry, the second time in two days and she couldn't remember the last time she'd cried before that. She hadn't even cried when she'd found Roger in bed with his bimbo. Mad at her weakness, she swiped the tears, and shoved the door open.

Blake met her at the bed of the truck, and they walked in silence to the elevator and then the apartment. She waited for him to search the apartment, and then joined him. She stood inside the door, trying to decide what to do, unsure how she felt. No, she wasn't unsure. She hurt. She hurt like she'd never hurt before.

Blake sat down on the couch and she walked into Royce's room, ignoring the rumpled sheets and the spicy male scent of the man she knew she loved, the man she'd always known would break her heart, and gathered as many of her things as would fit in a bag. She needed space, she needed to think. She needed trust.

She walked out of the bedroom, heading to the spare room down a hallway to the left of the master. Blake was watching the news, and he didn't look up, but when she was about to turn down the hall, the television went off.

"Lauren."

She paused without turning. "I meant it when I said 'what if destroys. It's the bitch of all bitches. Don't give her a chance to destroy you, or my brother."

CHAPTER
EIGHTEEN

Lauren's cell phone alarm buzzed near her head and her lashes shot open. She'd dozed off and on, but true deep sleep had never come. She turned off the alarm, emotion swelling insider her. Royce hadn't come to her, and it hurt, which confused her. She had told him to stay away. She wanted him to stay away. She sat up. Oh God. What if something had happened? What if he never came home? She shot to her feet, tugging her long pajama top to her knees as she hurried down the hall and rounded the wall, to stop dead in her tracks. Royce and Blake were both there, fully dressed and sleeping, the two chairs they occupied reclined back, the television on mute.

Lauren stared at Royce, his long hair half out of the clasp at his neck, the long, dark strands brushing his handsome, tension etched face. She inhaled and started to tiptoe to his bedroom, where she'd realized last night she'd left her purse and makeup, and pretty much everything she needed to get ready for work. She crept into his room, gently eased the door shut and then rushed to the bathroom.

Minutes later, she stepped into the shower, the hot water pouring relief into her stiff, tired muscles. She lingered, taking her time, not eager to get out and face the day, most likely filled with police and news people.

Finally, she forced herself to turn off the shower and pulled the curtain back. Royce sat on the toilet. Lauren jumped and let out a tiny yelp. He handed her a towel, his eyes lowered. She accepted it and wrapped it around herself.

His gaze lifted to hers, his eyes so blue, so tormented, they stole her breath. "I couldn't go to bed knowing you weren't there."

She squeezed her lashes shut, water dripping down her cheeks, off her hair. "I can't do this now. Not before I go to work." She stepped out of the tub and he wrapped his arms around her, pulled her close. "I wanted to tell you. I was going to tell you. I wasn't about to let your father hold this over my head for the rest of our lives. I—"

She shoved away from him, suddenly furious. This was about her father. "Right. You wouldn't want my father to hold this over your head." She pointed at the door. "I know this is your bathroom but please leave and let me get dressed. Please. I need to be alone."

"You took that wrong. You didn't—"

"I don't want to hear this now, Royce. I want to go to work and do what I do far better than relationships. I put criminals behind bars."

He studied her a long moment and then scrubbed his heavily stubbled jaw and stood up, towering over her. His eyes pierced hers, lingering on her face for several tense seconds, before he turned and walked away. She stood there, unable to move, in a puddle of water, and then something snapped inside her. She ran after him, rounding the bathroom door at the same moment he reached for the bedroom door.

"Consider yourself fired."

He turned to look at her. "You can't fire me. You didn't hire me and neither did your father, Lauren. I promised to check out a threat. I fell in love. The end." He turned and yanked open the door and left, slamming it behind him.

Lauren sank down on the floor and damn it, she was flipping crying again. He didn't love her. No. And saying he did was manipulative and mean. She was so damn tired of the men in her life using her like some sort of token. She swiped angrily at the stupid tears she should be above and forced herself to stand up. It was time she took a real lesson from Julie, that she separated sex from relationships, accepted that the relationship part was better left for people who liked heartache, because she didn't.

***

Royce showered in the spare bathroom and changed into jeans and a black t-shirt he'd left in his dryer, and was pulling on a leather jacket when the bedroom door opened. Lauren emerged, dressed in a cream colored suit that grabbed the highlights in her long, brown hair and turned them to sunshine. Hair he knew smelled like honey and vanilla. God, he had it bad for this woman and she hated him. He was pathetic, the kind of pathetic he would have called foolish in any other man.

"Ready?" he asked.

"You're taking me?"

"That's right, sweetheart," he said, and there was a bite to his voice he couldn't hide. She had a fist around his heart and just kept squeezing. "You're stuck with me until I catch your would-be killer. Then you can kick me to the curb."

She stared at him a long moment and then cut her gaze, her shoulders folding in slightly, that sunshine hair hiding her face. Emotion rolled off of her and punched him in the gut, twisting him in guilty knots.

"Lauren," he said softly.

Her gaze lifted to his. "Yes?"

"Truce, baby. Today is going to be hell. Let's be on the same team so we can get this SOB and make him pay."

"Yes," she said, a slight tremble to her voice. "Yes, okay." She walked toward him but they didn't speak.

They walked to the truck in silence, the tension between them so thick it might as well have been concrete. He helped her into the vehicle, their glances catching, the awareness between them crackling in the air. She still cared about him; he saw that in her eyes and determination filled him. He was going to make things right.

Fifteen minutes later, he parked at a meter in front of her office. "What are you doing?" she asked. "Aren't you just dropping me off?"

"Not today. Whoever this is saw us fight last night, or I'll gamble that he did, which means we need to send a clear message. I'm still here and I'm not going anywhere. I'm going to walk you in and I'm going to kiss you goodbye in public."

"That's... that's not necessary."

He reached for her and pulled her into his arms. "I love you, Lauren. I have since the moment I met you. I can't be mad at your father for bringing us together."

She dropped her head to his chest. "I'm afraid to believe you."

He tilted her chin up, gently forced her to look at him. "Then I'll show you and tell you until you do."

And when he expected her to push him away, she whispered. "Promise?"

Relief washed over him and he kissed her, a deep, passionate kiss and it took everything inside him to end it. "I promise."

"I'm not going to tell you I love you now," she said.

"Now?"

"Not now."

"If there's a later, I can live with that." He wiped smudged lipstick from her cheek. "The police aren't involved. I used my FBI contacts and they claimed jurisdiction and sealed the file. No press, and I have a guy over there working this already. He's simply no longer doing it off the books. He's a good man. This will be kept quiet."

Tension rushed from her body. "Thank you, Royce."

"Thank me by being safe. It's Tuesday. Your jury selection is still scheduled for tomorrow, right?"

"Yes."

"Okay, then I'm going to work through the evidence from last night before tomorrow. I have a feeling our guy will show up for that. I have three men on the building. I'm one phone call away. If you feel even a tiny bit uncomfortable, you call and I'm here. I'll take you home."

Her phone rang, she dug it out of her purse and he watched her hit 'ignore'. She glanced up at him. "My father. According to his five messages, he wants me to drop this case before I get 'everyone killed.'"

For once he was beginning to agree with the senator, and for his own selfish reasons. He wanted Lauren safe. "I'll walk you upstairs and I'll pick you up inside your office."

***

Several hours later Lauren had finally managed to focus on her work, and was deep in concentration when the buzzer on her desk made her jump. She hit the button.

"Lauren?"

"Oh God, I know that tone to your voice. Who is here that I don't want to see?"

"Mommie Dearest," she whispered.

"What? Why in the world... Sharon is here?"

"Oh yes."

This was odd and unexpected. "Fine. Send her in."

"Good luck."

Yeah, I'll need it, Lauren thought. Obviously Sharon wanted something. It was the only time she heard from the woman. Dropping her pen on the desk, she leaned back in her chair, hands settling on the arms rests.

Dressed from head to toe in Chanel, her skirt short and fitted, her perfume obnoxious, Sharon sashayed into the office.

"Hello, darling," she purred. "How is my favorite stepdaughter?"

"I'm your only stepdaughter," Lauren reminded her.

"Yes, dear, and that makes it even more special now, doesn't it?" She set her purse on a nearby chair, and moved to a decorative mirror on Lauren's wall, inspecting her appearance.

"What is it you want, Sharon?" Lauren asked without any effort to hide her impatience. "I have a lot on my plate today."

Dabbing at her lipstick first, obviously in no hurry, Sharon turned with a heavy sigh. "I want to talk about Brad."

"Brad. The house had a bomb in it last night and you want to talk about Brad."

"I want to talk about getting your life back on track. Clearly, you're spinning out of control and taking the rest of us with you." She sat down and crossed her legs. "And it seems to me that now, right after you almost got us all killed, is the perfect time to talk about real change. Quit this fool's game you play in this place and get serious about a bigger picture. Your father is being urged to run for the Republic presidential card again this term. He's seriously considering it, but to get the backing he needs, and that will be a massive cash influx, we must be solid as a family. This is a greater calling, a way to change the world. We all must make sacrifices, which means you have to stop this thing you do here and now. Battered women deserve sympathy, not the electric chair. You are making your father look bad."

Lauren stood up. "This conversation is over."

Sharon didn't get up. "I've talked to a consultant who thinks you and Brad being pulled together by family tragedy, the loss of your mother, of course, would be a story that warms hearts. It would show love found in the midst of pain. It would talk to the public."

"Are you crazy? Is your consultant crazy? That's practically incest."

Sharon waved that away. "You lived in the same household for a flutter of a moment and you are not blood related. It's a fairy tale."

"Does my father know this?"

"Of course not. He is too stressed. I told him I'd do everything. I'd clear the path to the oval office and find the money. All he has to do is focus on his political strategy."

"This ridiculous, insane conversation is over. I truly think you've finally proven to me you are not completely of this world, Sharon."

"Sit down, Lauren," she said sharply. "We are not done. Not even close."

Lauren glanced at her watch. "I have a meeting with my boss in ten minutes. I need to freshen up and get going." Grabbing her purse, Lauren waved toward the door. "I'll walk you out on my way to the washroom."

Sharon drew in a breath, her eyes blazing fire. "Fine. I'll talk to your father. Expect his call." She turned and marched for the door.

Lauren followed her to the door and watched her leave. "*Queen Bitch*," Alice mumbled, standing up and fluffing her gray hair. "I'm going to the mail room. That new supervisor needs to ask me a question."

Lauren smiled weakly, aware of Alice's crush. "Enjoy. I'm headed to my meeting." She followed Alice to the hallway and then stopped in the bathroom, happy to find it empty. She paused at the mirror, her fingers trailing over her lips, her mind replaying Royce's kiss, his words. *I love you, Lauren.*

She was just told to stop fighting for what she cared about, for what she thought was right and wrong in this world. Last night, this morning, she'd almost done that with Royce. The one person, other than his brothers, who had told her to keep going, who believed in what she did, in who she was. *He* felt right. He felt worth the risk. And he already had her heart. There was no sense trying to protect it. "I love you, too," she whispered, unable to deny the truth.

Feeling remarkably better considering the threats, the bomb, and a stepmother who was probably mentally ill, she headed for the door when the fire alarm went off. Oh good grief, not again. These test runs the building did disrupted everything. She reached for the door and then frowned. It didn't open. She tried again and it didn't move. Dropping her purse to the ground she tugged with two hands. Nothing.

Suddenly, the alarm became a part of a new nightmare. What if the building really was on fire? Oh, God, it was. There was a fire, and she was going to die. She grabbed her purse and scrambled for her phone, then hit auto-dial for Royce. No signal. She hit every auto-dial he'd put in her phone. Nothing. She was trapped in a burning building.

CHAPTER
NINETEEN

Royce had barely made it back to his building and sat down at his desk in the Walker office when Blake sauntered in, his long hair damp and slicked back, his stubble dark and unattended.

"Nice shave," Royce commented.

"I showered. I changed. I'm staying here today. This is as good as it gets." He sat down at one of the four steel desks in the office, directly across from Royce, leaned back in his chair, and kicked his boots up on the top.

"Morning, angels," Luke said, shoving through the door, his short hair neatly groomed, his face clean shaven.

Blake glanced over his shoulder at him. "Oh, yes. Morning, angel. Kiss, kiss, and cheery sunshine happiness to you." He grumbled something under his breath and then said, "I just heard from my ATF contact."

"And?" Royce and Luke asked at the same time, as Luke sat down on the edge of Blake's desk.

"You know from last night that the package had an amateur grade explosive device," Blake said. "The interesting part though, is that it had a timer. It's possible that it went off at the incorrect hour with a malfunction. But," he sat up, "think about this. A package that went off in the middle of the night when everyone was asleep. A snake that wasn't poisonous. And this bomb wasn't directed at Lauren."

"Two days before she starts jury selection," Royce commented.

"Right," Luke said. "She hasn't scared off yet, so the pressure increases."

"This doesn't mean she's not in danger," Blake said. "This could be some sadistic bastard who wants to torment her before he kills her."

Royce shot him a glowering look. "Thanks for the ice water in the face."

"Anytime, bro," Blake said.

"Could be a sick obsession with her," Luke said. "This guy—"

"Or woman," Royce inserted. "It could be a woman."

"Either way," Luke said, going back to his prior thought. "He filmed her. He followed her. He watched her."

Royce pushed to his feet and walked to the glass door of the small office, the only window to the street, staring out at the people passing by without seeing them. The clear way this person was stalking Lauren was eating him alive. "And we have nothing but a long list of suspects," Royce murmured, half to himself, before turning. "We need an end game, damn it. We need it now."

"We know he, or she, is after Lauren," Blake said. "Make her bait. Set her up in the open in a way that doesn't seem planned and bring him to her."

"Oh, what the fuck, Blake?" Royce said, stepping toward him, anger curling inside him ready to explode.

Blake jumped to his feet and met Royce toe-to-toe. "End this, Royce. End it before this SOB ends it for her and us."

Luke stepped between them, hands on both of their chest. "Enough. This does us no good."

"Damn it, Blake," Royce said, ignoring Luke. "This isn't the woman you love or you wouldn't say shit like that."

"No," Blake hissed as if burned. "The woman I loved is dead. I don't want Lauren to join her."

Royce felt the slap of those words, the instant deflation of his temper. He scrubbed his face and turned back to the glass door, pressing his hands to the surface, feeling more helpless than he'd felt in his entire FBI career.

"Let's just eliminate suspects," Luke suggested. "Sheridan's brother is in Germany. He's not our guy unless he contracted a professional."

"Which means he could still be our guy," Blake said, the chair creaking with his weight. "The one who can call off a contract to kill Lauren, if one exists. Anyone could have contracted a professional. That means the list is too damn long to do this. We aren't going to get answers quick enough. Gamble on the trial. It's about this week, about what is current and what is now."

"Sheridan's execution," Luke started.

"Has been minutes from happening several times before now," Blake argued, "and nothing happened. This is about *this trial*."

"He's right," Royce said, turning around, his gaze touching Blake's. "You're right. It's about the trial. Everything else is a diversion."

"The trial could be the diversion," Luke countered. "I don't think being short sighted is the answer here."

"Who has the most to lose or gain from this trial or the diversion it might cause?" Blake asked. "The top three names that come to your mind, Royce."

"The brother," Royce said. "He hates her. If I had to gamble, I'd put his name in all three spots."

"I put a man on him after you visited him," Luke said. "We have nothing to say he's the one. Nothing."

"It's him," Royce said. "And he knows he's being watched. You can count on it." He glanced at Luke. "Did we get his military record?"

"I've tried," he said. "It's being guarded tightly which tells me he's a very bad dude, or he's so damn good that he's involved with some deep government shit."

"Or both," Royce said.

Luke's cell phone rang and he answered it, then snapped it shut. "Lauren's building is being evacuated. People are pouring out of it."

"Lauren?"

"The crush of people is too intense," Luke said. "Our guys are working with the building security and the police to locate her."

Royce was pushing open the glass door before Luke ever finished the sentence, not about to risk New York traffic delays to get to Lauren. He dialed her phone, cursing himself for trusting someone else to protect her.

"I'm coming with you," Blake said following on his heels. "If it's a bomb again, I want to be there."

Royce cursed and shoved his phone back to his belt. "Her phone went straight to voice mail." He cut to the left and down the subway stairs.

"We have three men there," Blake told him, keeping pace. "She's okay."

"I should never have left her with someone else," he said, piling into the crush of people inside a car.

The next six minutes in the tunnel were hell for Royce. The car stopped and he burst out of the door and jumped the exit gates, Blake by his side. It was a block to the building and the instant Royce brought the fire trucks and police cars into view, he cursed and picked up speed, heading for the yellow tape and the gaggle of officials.

"I'm going in in case she's still up there," Royce shouted, his gut telling him she was in there, that she needed him.

"I'll deal with the Stroboscope," Blake called, "and I'll call you if I find her down here."

Royce targeted an entry point without officials and ducked the tape, wondering where the hell his other three men were. Someone shouted at him, but he didn't stop. He climbed the stairs to the building, burst through the glass doors, and instantly spotted Kyle.

Kyle, who knew how to work his connections, headed towards him immediately. "It was a bomb threat," he said. "A special team is already working the building."

"Where is she?"

"Daniel got positive confirmation from a cop that she was outside but when he got to the place he was told he could find her, she wasn't there. He can't find anyone who even saw her. Daniel and Rick are searching the crowd. I was about to hit the stairs to go up to look for her. The elevators are shut down."

Royce started to walk backwards, towards the stairwell. "Call

Blake. He's outside. Tell him what's going on." He turned and started running, yanking open the heavy steel door and charging upward. Every step was torture, another obstacle to getting to Lauren.

Ten floors later, he pulled the Glock from his ankle holster and eased the door open. Nothing. No one in sight and there was complete silence. His cell phone vibrated and he looked at the caller ID and answered. "Tell me you found her, Blake."

"No, get in and get her out. This guy has proven he knows explosive devices. Don't fuck around, Royce."

Royce hung up and shouted, "Lauren!" To hell with caution. Blake was right. If there really was a bomb, time was everything. He was halfway to her office when he paused, hearing a muffled pounding noise.

"Lauren!"

More pounding. He ran toward the noise, and then, thank God, he was at the bathroom door and heard the sweet sound of her voice. "Royce! I'm in here! Help. Please, help me."

"I'm here, baby. I'm here."

"Oh God, thank you. The door is stuck and my phone won't work, and—"

"But you're okay?" he asked, his gaze catching on the wooden doorstop jammed in the door.

"Yes. Yes. Now that you're here."

He yanked out the wedge and tossed it, pulling open the door. Lauren fell into his arms and clung to him as if he was her lifeline. Wrapping his arms around her, he hugged her, saying a silent thank you and kissing her. "Let's get out of here." He grabbed her hand and pulled her with him, his gun still at his side.

"What's happening?" she asked from behind him. "What's going on?"

"Bomb threat," he said, pulling open the door again and inspecting the path before pushing her in ahead of him. "In other words, run, don't walk down." He followed her, ready for a strike from behind.

***

Luke was standing inside the yellow line, talking to an official when he saw Julie shoving through the crowd, desperately trying to get to him. "Luke! Luke!"

"I'll be back," he said to the cop, heading to the tape to meet her, the pale pink of her fall jacket flaring behind her.

"Tell me she's okay," she pleaded, grabbing his arm. The touch sent that familiar punch to his gut that he'd always felt when she touched him, magnified by about ten because he knew Lauren was all she had, because he knew how scared she was.

"Royce went in after her," he said. "She'll be okay."

"Oh, God. So she really is still inside? They said there might be a bomb. Please tell me she isn't in there with a bomb."

"They just located it on the roof," he said. "A team's already tearing it down."

"But it's still live and she's still in there?" Her hand tightened on his arm. "Please tell me they already disarmed it."

"She'll be fine," he said, praying that was true, on edge himself about Royce getting the hell out himself. "He'll get her out, if she's even in there. If you want to help, search the crowd."

"I have," she said, swiping at a long lock of blond hair covering her face, her hand shaking. "I tried. I've looked. No one has seen her." She inhaled and let it out. "I don't... I can't lose her."

The vulnerability in her gave him another kick to the gut. He knew better than anyone, besides maybe Lauren, that Julie hid everything behind sex, sin, and a façade of cool, all of which were gone now.

"Hey," he said, bending under the tape to stand closer to her. "You won't." He reached up and slid the wayward hair in her eyes behind her ear. "You won't lose her."

They stared at each other, the past between them, the passion, the connection, and yes, even the bad goodbye, sizzling into awareness.

Her perfect pink lips parted, then, "Luke, I... we..."

A loud commotion erupted and they both turned to the building to find Royce and Lauren running toward them. Julie took a step closer to the tape, but then stopped and blinked up at Luke. Then, to his surprise, she pushed to her toes, and pressed her lips to his. "Thank you," she whispered and then ducked under the tape to run after Lauren.

Luke watched her embrace Lauren, savoring her taste on his lips, her scent on his skin while he did. And he knew right then that the wall he'd just seen come down had to fall again, and this time for good... and for him.

***

Hours later, when the bomb was disabled and she'd answered a million and one questions from law enforcement, Lauren walked into Royce's apartment, exhausted as the rush of adrenaline slid away. Royce tossed his keys on a small table by the door and

Lauren kicked off her heels, heading for the couch where she collapsed, thankful that her offices were closed the next day. Thankful that the trial would finally be ramping up for jury selection soon, and she could get this behind her.

Royce shoved the coffee table away and went down on his knees in front of her. "We have to talk, Lauren."

"Not the talk thing again," she said, sitting up to rest her hands on his chest. "It's never good and I can't deal with any more bad right now."

"Plead the case."

"What?" she asked, trying to scoot away from him. "No. You said you supported what I do and why I do it." She tried to scoot away from him.

He closed his hands on her hips and held her. "I do, but there is a time when everyone in law enforcement makes a decision, for the safety of everyone involved. This is one of those times."

"This is going to go public," she said. "Too many people know what is going on after today. That means the public will know a plea is caving to intimidation. What message does that send about our system? And it invites copycats. I'll be a target and make other people targets."

"You already are a target and other people are targets as well. Plead, Lauren. Put her away for life and make the concessions to do it. Then let's go away for a vacation. Rome, England, anywhere you want to go, and let Luke and Blake catch this guy."

"I can't believe you're asking me to do this. I thought…"

He kissed her, his fingers resting on her cheek. "I love you, Lauren. I'm just trying to protect you and everyone around you."

She softened instantly at the sincerity, the torment, in his voice and pressed her lips to his. "I love you, too."

He pulled back to search her face. "Then do this for me. I support you, baby. I believe in what you do, I do. But this is about safety."

"What if it isn't even about this case? We have clippings from other cases and the links to Sheridan."

"Then it's not this case and we've ruled it out. We have nothing at this point but a gamble, but we have to take it, Lauren."

"I need to think, Royce. I need to—"

He kissed her. "Think. That's better than 'no'." He slid his fingers under her hair to her neck. "Tell me you love me again."

She softened, smiled. "I love you."

He covered her mouth with his, as if he was trying to absorb the words, as if he cherished them. Lauren relaxed into the kiss, lost in him, letting herself forget everything but him undressing her, touching her, kissing her. When she finally straddled him, when he was buried deep inside her, and their eyes connected, she realized that her big, grizzly alpha had a soft side he saved just for her. And somehow, for just this little bleep of time, it made everything okay, and no man had ever done that for her before now, before Royce.

***

The next morning, Lauren woke in Royce's arms, to her cell phone ringing on the bedside table. He grabbed it and handed it to her.

She frowned at Caller ID. "It's the DA. This can't be good."

She answered, to hear her boss, Milton Waters demand, "Where are you? I'm at your apartment and you aren't here."

"You're at my... why?"

"I received a delivery for you this morning," he said. "Where are you?"

Royce rolled out of bed when she gave him the address. "Any clue what's going on?"

She headed to the closet. "He's going to tell me to plea."

"Did he say that?"

She yanked a pink t-shirt from a hanger in his closet, that was beginning to feel like hers, clinging to that little piece of goodness in the midst of a whole lot of hell.

By the time Lauren had dressed in jeans and pulled on boots, Royce was leading Milton to his living room. The District Attorney, forty-something, good looking, and dressed in his standard black suit and red tie, was crackling with anger. "I'm having the trial date postponed a week. Plead the case."

She crossed her arms in front of her. "Milton..."

"The Mayor wants the case done. I want this case done. I only let you ride this out because the victim's family took it to the news."

"Not because the woman murdered her husband," Lauren said. "Of course not."

"The public, and the jury, will be sympathetic to her," he said. "They won't be when we get a building full of people killed and I did nothing to stop it."

Lauren took that like a punch in the gut. "If we plead it out now, you'll look weak and we'll invite other attacks. You'll risk your office falling apart, and on an election year to boot."

He considered her a long moment. "You tell the opposing

council to give us something to work with, a piece of this puzzle that justifies the deal we swore wasn't happening. Then you plead the damn thing and do it by Monday." He headed for the door and stopped and turned. "And I'm going to let the media know that there is new evidence, and plead talks are in the works. So you damn sure better come up with a good follow up story to justify this. I'm in this because of you."

Lauren stood there, staring after him, unmoving even when the door slammed shut. Royce pulled her into his arms. "Baby."

She pushed away from him. "No. Don't. You want this too. Everyone wants this. I don't know why I fight like this. I don't know why I think that what is right matters when no one else does. I need to go call Mark."

He looked like he might argue, but then nodded, stepping back. "Just remember his reasons aren't mine."

She scraped her teeth over her lip, chest tight. "I know. I do. I don't mean to lash out at you. I'm just upset and confused and I just don't know what I'm doing anymore. But I know I can't keep this up. I can't leave Julie in a hotel. I can't put other people at risk. It just feels like this was all for nothing."

"I'm here when you need me."

Her lashes lowered and lifted. "I know and it matters." She headed to the kitchen, taking her phone and some paperwork with her, before sitting down at the table.

A few minutes later, she was deep in conversation with Mark. "I'll get you what you need," he said, pausing a moment. "Look. I'm happy to get my deal, but let's put that aside. You'll never get to fight for what you believe in in the public sector. Lindsey and I have been talking about you. We want you to come work for us. Or go out on your own, Lauren, or with Julie.

Just get the hell out from under that asshole Milton."

She sank back into the chair. "Until this week, I think I would have said 'no.' I would have thought I was caving to the pressure and giving up on my beliefs."

"Is that a 'yes'?"

"It's an 'I'll think about it.' Seriously. I'll think about it seriously."

"I'll take that," he said. "Are you going to the annual Children's Charity event at the museum? Lindsey and I will be there and we can talk."

Oh, God. Julie coordinated the event every year and not without pain, and this time, while stuck in a hotel. "Yes. Probably." If she could go without putting everyone at risk.

"Great. I'll look for you. And how about I get you this plea information today, and we just get it behind us?"

"Email it," she said. "And yes. Now that I've decided to do this, let's be done with it." She ended the call and noted the missed call from her father.

Lauren sighed and called him back, listening to half an hour of him telling her all the reasons she should quit her job. He almost talked her into keeping her job, when he said, "You can be my legal counsel for the Presidential campaign."

"I'm sure Brad and Roger have that handled," she said.

"We need you too, Lauren," he said. "Running for the nomination is going to be a family affair. We might as well stand united."

She could almost hear her stepmother in his words. "I support you, Father, but in the background."

When they finally hung up, she sat there, staring into space, replaying the conversation, and telling herself not to let it impact her decision.

"You okay?"

Her gaze went to the doorway, to where Royce sauntered towards her, too graceful for such a large man, his long hair loose around his shoulders.

She pushed to her feet and wrapped her arms around his neck. "Mark wants to hire me and my father wants me to quit my job and join his campaign. Oh, and Julie has a huge charity event at the museum Saturday night that I am now afraid to go to for fear I will turn it into 'Nightmare in the Museum.'"

"Let's see how the next few days go, and decide about the event. As for the jobs," his strong arm circled her waist, "what do you want?"

She didn't know anymore. "You," she said. "I want you to help me forget all of this."

He scooped her up and headed for the bedroom, where she planned to stay as long as she could possibly keep him there.

Her dress was sexy as sin, a long, cream colored number that Julie had brought her, and it hugged every sleek line of her body. Just another reason Royce wanted to turn away from the museum before he pulled the truck into the valet parking. He didn't care that Saturday night had come with no more threats, that the plea had seemed to end the hell. The bastard was still out there, still a ghost they couldn't find, and he wasn't going to rest until they found him. This had ended too easily, and too easy, he'd learned, was never easy at all. It was the calm before a storm, but he wasn't going to put Lauren on edge again. He damn sure didn't tell her that he was so antsy about this event that he had Blake and Luke in a surveillance van a block away. When tonight was over, he was going to present her with tickets to Rome, and they were getting the heck out of Dodge until he knew this was really over.

"You sure you don't want to just skip this?" he asked her for the third time since he'd shackled himself into a monkey suit, otherwise known as a tuxedo.

"No, Royce," she said. "You know I have to be there for Julie. I put her through living in a hotel for days. I have to show my support. She's family. And she bought me this dress."

He sighed and turned into the drive. "I do owe her for that one. I like it."

She laughed. "So you keep telling me. I'm sure Sharon will call it inappropriate, when her own dress will be far more so." She shrugged out of her coat and the valet opened her door.

Royce quickly exited and handed off the keys before stepping to her side, wrapping his arm around her as she shivered. "I'm going to have to give up this tux jacket. You're going to be cold inside."

"You just want an excuse to give it up," she said. "And you have to wear it."

They waited by the door, as several other people entered before them. Suddenly, cameras started to flash around them and a reporter stepped close to them. "Is it true your father is running for the Republican nomination, Ms. Reynolds?"

"That's a question for him," she said quickly.

"Is that why you caved to a plea deal for the husband killer?"

She stopped walking, the color draining out of her face.

Royce pulled her to the other side of him and forward, inside the building. The minute they were inside and signed the register, he pulled her aside. "Blow that off, baby. It means nothing. If that's the worst thing that happens tonight, we're good." His hand brushed her bare shoulder. "The best thing, at least for me, is going to be peeling this dress off of you." He motioned to the room. "Let's go mingle so I can get to do it sooner rather than later."

She laughed, a soft, sexy sound that he'd never get tired of hearing, and wrapped her arm around him. They entered an oval room with doorways leading to art displays, towering ceilings and several winding stairwells that led to the balcony areas above. Displays of food and drink framed tables and chairs with white tablecloths.

Julie hurried toward them, dressed in a long light blue silk dress that accented her voluptuous curves that Royce was pretty sure Luke would approve of, even if his brother wouldn't admit it.

"Hey, sweetie," Julie said, hugging Lauren. "How are you?" She looked at Lauren's arm where the burn mark was covered by a bandage. "Stylish and sexy. Does it hurt?"

"No, not anymore," Lauren said, and then added, "And it's not like I could hide it in this particular dress."

"Which I should thank you for buying," Royce quickly added.

Julie winked. "My pleasure and yours too, I hope." Then to Lauren, she said, "I have to mingle. Mark and Lindsey are looking for you. They are at a center table. Mommy Dearest is shopping the art, and your father is on his way. Brother Brad is also present." She glanced up. "Judge Moore and his wife are here. Talk about awkward." She lowered her voice, "I'm serving her divorce papers Monday."

Lauren gaped. "And he's with her tonight?"

"Yeah. He's a cold-hearted bastard, that one." She plastered on a fake smile. "Off to act friendly."

Someone cleared their throat from behind them and Royce turned with Lauren's hand tucked under his elbow. Her stepbrother, whom Royce had met on several occasions, stood there, and Royce felt Lauren tense and melt closer to his side.

"Lauren," Brad said tightly, his gaze hitting Royce with a hostile blow. "I see you haven't disposed of your bodyguard."

A muscle in Royce's jaw jumped, but he kept his tone cool. "Seems there are all kinds of unsavory characters around her I need to protect her from."

Brad's eyes narrowed, sliding from Royce to Lauren and back. "She's making some statement to her father. Once she's done making it, you'll be done."

"What?" Lauren demanded. "I... I don't even know what to say to you."

"You say 'where's the bar?' and walk away," Royce offered, turning her away and urging her forward, before leaning in close. "And I'll be your statement any day of the week, as long as it's forever."

She stopped and looked up at him. "What?"

"I've got you now," he said. "I'm not letting you go. But we'll talk later."

The tension slid away from her. "Talk. You want to talk?" She rose up on her toes, and whispered in his ear, "Either you want me forever or you don't."

He wrapped his arm around her waist and kissed her, not giving a damn about propriety. "I want you. Forever." He trailed his fingers down her arm. "Let's find Mark before I forget why it matters and then drag you out of here."

She laughed and they quickly found Mark and his wife Lindsey, a dynamite blonde who was as gorgeous as she was friendly, and joined them at their table.

"So I hear Mark proposed a new career option for you," Lindsey said, getting right to the point.

"He said something about it, yes."

"So what do I have to do to talk you into it? I need some women power at the firm. I'm the only one there."

From there, Royce was pleased to see Lauren relax and get lost in conversation with Lindsey. Royce and Mark were both pleased to see the magic unfold, as Lindsey convinced Lauren that she had to join their firm.

A good hour passed before Lauren pushed to her feet and Royce followed her. "Bathroom," she said. "You talk your football. I want to find Julie, too, so I might be a few." She took off through the crowd.

He hesitated, fighting the urge to follow her, telling himself he was being paranoid. But whoever had been terrorizing her was still out there somewhere.

**

Lauren walked down the hallway into the ladies, feeling more relaxed than she had in a very long time, a smile touching her lips. She was in love and she was no longer being stalked. And, damn it, she was going to quit her job and join Mark and Lindsey, and if she could talk Julie into leaving the firm she was with, she'd get her on the boat, too.

She turned a corner to enter the bathroom when Sharon stepped in front of her, her black dress twinkling in the overhead lights. "Let's step to the courtyard and talk."

"It's cold, Sharon, and I have to get back to my table."

"I received an interesting delivery today," she said. "You're going to want to know what's inside and not where others can see it."

Lauren's lips parted in shock. This couldn't be happening. There couldn't be yet another threat. "Okay. Let's go."

"I thought so," Sharon said smugly and turned and headed

down the hall, away from the main room.

Lauren balled her fists at her sides and followed, telling herself not to overreact. Sharon was notorious for her ridiculous reactions to things. She opened the door, the cool fall night chilling her skin.

Greenery and trees lined a red brick path that allowed guests to go forward, left or right.

"We'll want to walk further into the courtyard," Sharon said, flicking her a hard look. "We don't need an audience."

Lauren hesitated a second, before following again, not comfortable with the secluded location, which was ridiculous. Sharon was a bit off her rocker, but she wasn't dangerous. A few people milled around at the concrete seats along the way, and while that should have eased Lauren's unease, it didn't.

Sharon walked up the steps of the gazebo, a slim heater hanging from the ceiling and down to almost the floor, sending Lauren in pursuit a bit more eagerly. Lauren rushed to the glowing device and held her hands above it. A second later, someone grabbed her from behind and she blacked out.

***

Twenty minutes after Lauren left the table Royce was talking football with Mark when he saw Julie nearby and stopped mid-sentence. Lauren wasn't with her.

"Give me a minute, Mark," he said, pushing to his feet and going to Julie's side. "Where's Lauren?"

"I don't know. I thought she was with you. Is something wrong?"

"She went to the bathroom and was supposed to be finding

you. I need you to—"

"I'm going," she said, heading for the bathroom without another word. Royce fell into step with her, his adrenaline pumping, telling himself to stay calm. She was okay.

"Has her father arrived?"

"If he has I haven't seen him," she said, as they rounded the corner to the bathroom. "But maybe that's because they are off talking. She'd been avoiding him." She pushed the bathroom door open and went inside.

Royce's cell phone rang and he yanked it off his belt to see Blake in the Caller ID. He answered and Blake immediately said, "Is Lauren with you?"

"No, I can't find her."

"Front door," Blake said. "Now."

"She's not here," Julie said, rushing out of the bathroom.

Royce turned away from her, charging for the door, and barely keeping himself from running. He was in front of the building in a minute flat and the van was waiting.

The side door opened. "Get in," Blake said and Royce didn't ask questions.

Royce was inside and the van moving before the door was even shut, Luke taking off like a bat out of hell. He rotated on his heels to find the computer panel on the wall lit up with a tracking program, a dot beeping.

"That's Lauren," Blake said. "That chip you put in her watch wasn't working. I found the problem. Now it's working. Luke has the feed up front, too."

Royce inhaled a calming breath, and letting it out. "What else do we know?"

"Not a damn thing."

"Exiting towards the Bronx," Luke shouted.

Royce headed to the front with Luke, willing the van to move quicker, and cursing the traffic that had them at a dead stop… afraid Lauren would be dead before he got to her.

CHAPTER
TWENTY-ONE

Lauren woke to a throbbing in her head and neck, lost in a fog she couldn't seem to escape.

"I don't understand why I'm here," a female said. "I'm not supposed to be involved. You said I wouldn't have to be involved. And what's the camera for?

"Better to see with, sweetheart."

The voices played in her head, her mind starting to process. Sharon. The female was Sharon. She tried to move and couldn't, panic overtaking her. Lauren jerked her head up and tugged on her arms to find her hands tied behind her back, behind the rails of a wooden chair.

Her gaze traveled frantically over a warehouse of some sort, and landed on the two people talking, their backs to her. Sharon and... Oh God. Wilkins, dressed in army fatigues with at least one gun and one knife attached to his hip. This wasn't happening. It couldn't be happening.

"Well, look who's awake," he said, turning to face her. "This would be no fun if you weren't fully present."

"I don't need to see this," Sharon said. "I don't. I need to get out of here. Take me out of here before you do it."

"It?" Lauren said. "What is it?"

"You're a smart person," he said, walking to her and squatting down beside her. "I'm pretty sure you can figure it out." He brushed his gloved fingers over her cheek and Lauren tried to pull away, pretty sure the gloves were a bad sign for her future. He laughed, as if her resistance amused him. "Pretty little thing, you are. I think Mama here hates you for that as much as she does anything else. We bonded over hating you that day I paid your father a visit. A romp in the sack later, a few bucks in my bank, and I got paid into scaring you into that plea. She's hot in the sack, a fucking wildcat your old fogie father can't keep up with."

"Shut up, Jonathan," she growled behind him. "Just shut up."

He flicked a look over his shoulder. "Who's she going to tell?" His eyes fixed on Lauren. "She's a wicked witch. I knew you wouldn't leave the DA, and you sure as hell wouldn't marry your stepbrother. That's some twisted shit." He pulled his gun and slid it to her chin.

"Please, don't do this," Lauren said, her voice shaking, her entire body shaking. "Please."

"We were always going to end up right here, with you and me," he said. "I knew that the day I visited your office." He pushed to his feet, walked to a video camera and adjusted it.

"Do you really think my father will run for office after I'm murdered?" Lauren demanded.

"I'll convince him he has to make the world a better place, in your honor, you little bitch," Sharon snapped. "And he'll win with the sympathy vote. You will give me the White House from the grave. I'll finally get something for putting up with you all these years."

Jonathan walked to Sharon and came up behind her. "What are you doing?" she demanded.

"Getting you ready for you big day," he said, pressing the gun into her hand. "You're going to shoot her yourself."

"No. No, I can't do it."

"You will," he said, stepping back from her and pointing another gun at her head. "You'll shoot her or I'll shoot you both."

"What?" Sharon screeched. "What are you doing?"

"Insurance, sweetheart," he said. "When you get to the White House you're going to get my sister pardoned or the world will know you murdered your stepdaughter."

He stepped backwards to the camera and she turned to him. "Turn around!" he shouted, cocking his gun. She started to shake and cry.

All Lauren could think of was how much she wished she'd told Royce how much she loved him, how alone Julie would be. How alone her father would be. "Don't do this, Sharon," Lauren said. "You have a gun just like him. Shoot him. Shoot him and I won't say a word about this."

Sharon whirled on Lauren, holding up the gun. "Shut up! Shut up! You are always talking." She cocked the gun.

Lauren squeezed her eyes shut and started to pray. Royce was going to blame himself, he was going to let it eat him alive. She didn't want that. She didn't... The sound of bullets rang out and she braced herself for impact, but nothing happened. Suddenly, Sharon was on the ground and so was Wilkins, and Royce was kneeling in front of her, his hands on her face.

"You're okay. You're okay, baby."

"Is she?"

"Dead," he said. "Yes."

Lauren burst into tears, shaking worse now than ever. Royce untied her and picked her up and she curled into him, not wanting to see Sharon's body. The sound of sirens erupted outside the building, as they the warehouse.

She had no concept of time, of when the chaos calmed and the EMS crew reluctantly released her. She knew though, that they had tried to convince her to go to the hospital to be treated for shock.

They walked to the van and paused by the passenger door. "I have to tell my father," she said.

"We'll do it together."

"I was hoping you'd say that."

"You don't ever have to do anything alone again," he promised. "I'm here and I swear to you, Lauren, I will never again let you down like I did tonight."

She flung her arms around him. "You didn't let me down. You saved my life. I love you. I don't know if I've really truly told you how much. I didn't tell my mother enough. I was a teenager, and it wasn't cool and then she was just gone. Tonight I almost died and my last thought was how much I wished I had told you how much you've changed my life, how much you mean to me."

"I love you, too, baby, more than you know. If you'd have died in there, I would have died with you." He ran his hand down her hair. "Let's go talk to your father. We'll get through the bad, and we'll make the good together."

EPILOGUE

A month after Lauren had sat in that wooden chair, certain she was going to die, she stood in a pink silk robe on a Paris balcony looking out over the city, appreciating life more than ever. The moon was full, the stars twinkling in a fairy tale vision of perfection.

She had two weeks of heaven here with Royce, and then she'd start her new job with Mark and Lindsey. Her father was retiring from government to run his own firm, and had fired Brad, though Roger was still around. Apparently, her father had been blackmailed, though she'd never found out about what. Just that he now knew that Sharon had been involved, and perhaps, though she wasn't certain, Brad as well.

Royce walked up behind her and slid his arms around her. "It's beautiful," he said, staring out at it with her.

"Yes," she sighed. "I'm so glad we did this."

"Me too, baby," he said, and turned her to face him. "And I can't think of a better time or place to have a talk."

She laughed and turned in his arms. "Not the talk again."

"Oh, yeah," he said. "The talk." His expression turned serious, and he added, "I can't go on like this, Lauren."

There was something so intense about him that her heart

skipped a beat. "What does that mean?"

"It means I want things to change between us." He went down on his knee and took her hand before presenting a black velvet box and flipping the lid open. "Forever, baby. Either you want me forever or you don't."

A gorgeous white diamond twinkled as brightly as the stars and her lips lifted in a smile. "On one condition. You still have to work on the bossy thing."

"You like the bossy thing."

"Sometimes," she admitted, and then bent down and kissed him. "Forever." He scooped her up in his true alpha glory, and took her to bed, where he excelled at being deliciously bossy.

THE END

The Tall, Dark and Deadly series
Book 1: Hot Secrets (Royce's story)
Book 2: Dangerous Secrets (Luke's story)
Book 3: Beneath the Secrets (Blake's story)

And coming April 7, 2016
A Tall, Dark and Deadly spinoff series:
WALKER SECURITY
Book 1: Deep Under (Kyle's story)

Want more BLAKE WALKER? Read the INSIDE OUT series in which he is a very prominent character and his brothers make an appearance too!

And now a sneak peek into IF I WERE YOU, book one in the New York Times bestselling INSIDE OUT series by Lisa Renee Jones

The INSIDE OUT series is now in development for television with producer Suzanne Todd (Alice in Wonderland, Must Love Dogs, Austin Powers, The Boiler Room, and more)

Stay tuned to Lisa's website for updates on the TV show!
www.lisareneejones.com

Excerpt from
IF I WERE YOU

We begin our walk, faster this time, and the cold wind has nothing on the chill between us. Conversation is non-existent, and I have no clue how to break the silence, or if I should even try. I dare a peek at his profile several times, fighting the wind blowing hair over my eyes, but he doesn't acknowledge me. Why won't he look at me? Several times, I open my mouth to speak but words simply won't leave my lips.

We are almost to the gallery, and a knot has formed in my stomach at the prospect of an awkward goodbye, when he suddenly grabs me and pulls me into a small enclave of a deserted office rental. Before I can fully grasp what is happening, I am against the wall, hidden from the street and he is in front of me, enclosing me in the tiny space. I blink up into his burning stare and I think I might combust. His scent, his warmth, his hard body, is all around me, but he is not touching me. I want him to touch me.

He presses his hand to the concrete wall above my head when I want it on my body. "You don't belong here, Sara."

The words are unexpected, a hard punch in the chest. "What? I don't understand."

"This job is wrong for you."

I shake my head. I don't belong? Coming from Chris, an established artist, I feel inferior, rejected. "You asked me why I wasn't following my heart. Why I wasn't pursuing what I love. I am. That's what I'm doing."

"I didn't think you'd do it in this place."

This place. I don't know what he's telling me. Does he mean this gallery? This city? Has he judged me not worthy of his inner circle?

"Look, Sara." He hesitates, and lifts his head to the sky, seeming to struggle for words before fixing me with a turbulent look. "I'm trying to protect you here. This world you've strayed into is filled with dark, messed up, arrogant assholes who will play with your mind and use you until there is nothing else left for you to recognize in yourself."

"Are you one of those dark, messed up, arrogant assholes?"

He stares down at me, and I barely recognize the hard lines of his face, the glint in his eyes, as belonging to the man I've just had lunch with. His gaze sweeps my lips, lingers, and the swell of response and longing in me is instant, overwhelming. He reaches up and strokes his thumb over my bottom lip. Every nerve ending in my body responds and it's all I can do not to touch him, to grab his hand, but something holds me back. I am lost in this man, in his stare, in some spellbinding, dark whirlwind of…what? Lust, desire, torment? Seconds tick eternally and so does the silence. I want to hold him, to stop whatever I sense is coming but I cannot.

"I'm worse." He pushes off the wall, and is gone. He is gone. I am alone against the wall, aching with a fire that has nothing to do with the meal we shared. My lashes flutter, my fingers touch my lip where he touched me. He has warned me away from Mark, from the gallery, from him, and he has failed. I cannot turn away. I am here and I am going nowhere.

IF I WERE YOU is available on all platforms. For more information, buy links and the INSIDE OUT reading order visit: www.lisareneejones.com

Also by Lisa Renee Jones

The Inside Out Series
If I Were You
Being Me
Revealing Us
His Secrets*
Rebecca's Lost Journals
The Master Undone*
My Hunger*
No In Between
My Control*
I Belong to You
All of Me*

The Secret Life of Amy Bensen
Escaping Reality
Infinite Possibilities
Forsaken
Unbroken*

Careless Whispers
Denial
Demand (May 2016)
Surrender (December 2016)

Dirty Money
Hard Rules (August 2016)
More information coming soon...

*eBook only

About the Author

New York Times and USA Today bestselling author Lisa Renee Jones is the author of the highly acclaimed INSIDE OUT series, which is now in development for a television show to be produced by Suzanne Todd of Team Todd (Alice in Wonderland). Suzanne Todd on the INSIDE OUT series: *Lisa has created a beautiful, complicated, and sensual world that is filled with intrigue and suspense. Sara's character is strong, flawed, complex, and sexy – a modern girl we all can identify with. I'm thrilled to develop a television show that will tell Sara's whole story – her life, her work, her friends, and her sexuality.*

In addition to the success of Lisa's INSIDE OUT series, she has published many successful titles. The TALL, DARK AND DEADLY series and THE SECRET LIFE OF AMY BENSEN series, both spent several months on a combination of the *New York Times* and USA Today bestselling lists. Lisa is presently working on a dark, edgy new series, Dirty Money, for St. Martin's Press.

Prior to publishing Lisa owned multi-state staffing agency that was recognized many times by The Austin Business Journal and also praised by the Dallas Women's Magazine. In 1998 Lisa was listed as the #7 growing women owned business in Entrepreneur Magazine.

Lisa loves to hear from her readers. You can reach her at www.lisareneejones.com and she is active on Twitter and Facebook daily.

CPSIA information can be obtained at www.ICGtesting.com
Printed in the USA
LVOW11s1532260616

494183LV00004B/318/P